Emma decided she was done fighting what she felt for Jamie.

She was tired of being strong, focused and directed all the time. More important, she was tired of being alone.

Not that she thought she'd found her soul mate or anything crazy like that. She believed the soul mate thing was as real as Big Foot—but Jamie made her laugh, something she hadn't done enough of since her mother got sick, and for right now, that was enough. No harm, no foul. And he'd been such a rock for her when she found out about Andrew. It would have been so easy to fall apart, and she probably would have if it hadn't been for Jamie.

He got out of Mick's battered Chevy truck, looking way too good for this early in the morning, wearing one of the shirts he'd bought when they'd gone shopping. As it happened, it was her favorite, the tan-and-brown plaid, which matched his coffee-colored eyes.

Before when he was dressed in khakis and a polo shirt he looked... She searched for the right word. *Restrained. Reserved.* Almost as if he were apart from everyone and everything around him here. Now a relaxed air surrounded him. He appeared at ease. Almost as if she was seeing the inner man for the first time. He looked as though he'd been here his entire life. As though he belonged.

She nodded toward his feet. "Good-looking boots."

"Do I pass muster?"

Talk about a stupid question. "You'll do."

Dear Reader,

This story took me on an unexpected journey, but then they often do. I knew I wanted to write about the struggle to find a career when life throws you a killer curve ball, but I discovered something else writing this story.

My youngest son was in the play *Big Love* at school while I wrote *A Cowboy in the Making*. The end of his character's speech made me tear up. "When push comes to shove and people need defending, no one wants a good guy anymore."

I thought about that. We all love a bad boy, but when life's crumbling around me, I want a guy I can rely on. A good guy. One who will step up and do what's needed without being asked. One who'll be there no matter what. That's the kind of guy Jamie Westland is.

For me, that's one of the appeals of a cowboy. He's a good guy with strong values who can be counted on to do what's right and will treat a woman as though she is special. I think sometimes a woman does want a good guy. At least I hope so, since that's what I keep telling my sons.

Stop by www.juliebenson.net to let me know your thoughts on the bad boy/good guy debate. I'd love to hear from you.

Blessings,

Julie

COWBOY IN THE MAKING

—

JULIE BENSON

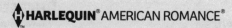

Recycling programs
for this product may
not exist in your area.

ISBN-13: 978-0-373-75537-0

COWBOY IN THE MAKING

Copyright © 2014 by Julie Benson

Printed in U.S.A.

ABOUT THE AUTHOR

An avid daydreamer since childhood, Julie always loved creating stories. After graduating from the University of Texas at Dallas with a degree in sociology, she worked as case manager before having her children: three boys. Many years later she started pursuing a writing career to challenge her mind and save her sanity. Now she writes full-time in Dallas, where she lives with her husband, their sons, two lovable black dogs, two guinea pigs, a turtle and a fish. When she finds a little quiet time, which isn't often, she enjoys making jewelry and reading a good book.

Books by Julie Benson

HARLEQUIN AMERICAN ROMANCE

For Jennifer Jacobson

Without your support, encouragement and musical expertise this book never would have been written. You are such a shining example of God's love here on earth, and I'm so blessed to have you in my life.

And thanks to the Starbucks crew at Custer and Renner in Richardson, especially Jason, Angel, Susan, Christine, Ashley (both of them!), Derek and Nate for keeping me caffeinated while I wrote this one. You're the best!

Chapter One

"I heard the bad news about the Philharmonic letting you go. How're you doing?"

James Westland's hand tightened around his cell phone as he tried to shove aside his growing irritation at his friend Connor's comment. What he wouldn't give for a call from a charity asking for a donation or a wrong number. He'd even be thrilled with an obscene call. Anything but a call from another friend or relative asking how he was holding up.

How the hell did everyone expect him to be when his career was becoming a distant spec in his rearview mirror? Of course he was pissed. At first he'd tried drowning his anger in a bottle of Jameson, but all that did was leave him with a bad hangover. Now he'd reached the not-sure-what-the-hell-to-do stage.

"I'm fine. I'm assessing my options." He almost laughed. *Right. You've got so many of those to choose from.*

Unlike his siblings, Jamie had never excelled in school. He'd studied twice as hard to earn low B's and C's. For their paltry efforts, his sisters had scored straight A's. One now possessed an MBA and the other a degree in engineering. Education that offered them more options, while he'd put all his career eggs into the music basket, leaving him little to fall back on now.

"My sister teaches at a private school in Manhattan," Connor said. "I could see if she knows of anyone who's looking for a music teacher."

"Sure," he said mainly out of ingrained politeness and because he couldn't afford to rule out any ideas at this point.

How could a simple Sunday morning bike ride have ended up turning his life upside down? He still had trouble letting go of the what-ifs.

What if I'd slept in? What if the guy in the parked car had been as concerned about the world around him as his coffee? Would he have opened the door and knocked me to the ground? What if I hadn't tried to break my fall? Would I have hurt my hand so bad?

"I don't know what I'd do if I couldn't play the cello anymore," Connor said, breaking through Jamie's thoughts.

There it was. The barely veiled invitation to spill his guts and say how angry he was or how he was falling apart. If anyone else hinted he was concerned he'd do something stupid like jump off the Brooklyn Bridge, he might throw his phone off said bridge.

His left hand cramped and he switched his phone to his right, staring at the offending appendage as if it should look different. How many people would be thrilled to have the mobility he possessed, and yet for him, it wasn't enough. "It's taking some adjusting to, but I'm managing."

"Maybe you should get away. Take some time to clear your head."

Or at least get away before the well-intentioned people in his life drove him insane. He considered visiting his parents in Philadelphia, but tossed the idea aside. While he loved them, they were planners. They analyzed a situation, determined the risks and probability of success for each option and then acted. That's what they'd want to do with this situation—provide him with a feasibility study. He couldn't take the in-person seminar right now. The phone version had been bad enough.

A picture of his grandfather's small ranch in the Rocky Mountains flashed in Jamie's mind. A simple two-story house straight out of a Norman Rockwell painting with a big old-fashioned porch with rocking chairs perfect for thinking. Going to Colorado was what he needed. There he could clear his head and sort things out.

Mick would understand what he was going through because he'd experienced the same uncertainty when he'd returned from Vietnam after shrapnel from a land mine had torn up his right leg, arm and hand, ending his own musical career. While he'd understand, Mick wouldn't pry. Nor would anyone else in Estes Park, because very few of the town's eight thousand residents knew more about him than that he was Mick's grandson.

Except Emma, but then, last he'd heard she was living in Nashville.

"Jamie, you still there?" Connor asked. "I wish there was something I could do."

Out of patience now that he had a plan, Jamie thanked his friend for checking about the teaching possibilities, ended the conversation and called Mick. When the old man answered, Jamie said, "Mind if I come for a visit?"

"The door's always open to you."

"Great. I'll be on a plane tomorrow."

"You know I'm not one to ask a lot of nosy questions, and tell me if I'm outta line doing it now. It won't hurt my feelings none, but I hear something in your voice so I gotta ask. Is something wrong?"

Unlike when others asked, Mick's question didn't irritate Jamie. "When you got hurt and couldn't perform, did everyone keep asking what you were going to do with your life?"

"Your hand didn't heal right," Mick said in a matter-of-fact voice.

"The doctor says everything looks fine, but when I play my hand doesn't work like it used to. My fingers get knotted up. The dexterity and flexibility just isn't there." Jamie explained how music he'd once played without conscious effort now proved difficult. To the untrained ear he might not sound too bad, but unless things changed, he wouldn't be returning to the Philharmonic anytime soon. "The doctor says there's a chance my hand will get better. He says strengthening may be all it needs."

Keep telling yourself that so you can hang on to the hope that your career isn't over.

"Nothing will do that better than good old-fashioned hard work around the ranch and the restaurant, and I've got plenty to do at both places. In fact, I could use a bartender."

"Making mixed drinks is an art form nowadays. That's out of my league."

Mick laughed. "Maybe in New York City, but most folks that come into my place aren't big on fancy mixed drinks. They order a beer on tap or in a bottle. Other than that it's pouring whiskey or making margaritas for the ladies. I can show you how to do that."

"I think I can handle that."

"Good. I'll see you tomorrow. Let me know when your flight gets in. I'll pick you up at the airport."

Jamie thought about telling Mick he'd rent a car, but right now he'd rather avoid the expense. He had some money in savings, but only enough to last a couple of months. Considering his uncertain future, best to be frugal.

"For what it's worth, I know what you're going through, and I wouldn't wish it on my worst enemy," Mick said. "It really knocked my feet out from under me for a while."

That's right where Jamie was. Flat on his back trying to figure out what to do once he found the energy to stand again.

"People didn't realize playing and singing were a part of me," Mick continued. "When I lost that, it was like a part of me died, and I had to grieve. Until I did, I couldn't move on. Most people didn't get that. They wanted to help, but their concern most times made it worse."

"Concern I can take. It's the pity that's pissing me off."

"Don't let this get you down, son. I know it seems bad now, but an unexpected blessing can find its way into situations like this."

Jamie shook his head. If there was something good in the midst of this mess, fate was doing a damned good job hiding the fact.

EMMA DONOVAN STARED at Molly, the fiddle player in her band, Maroon Peak Pass, standing in the doorway of her office at the Estes Park animal shelter.

There's a woman with bad news to deliver.

"I can't do this anymore, Em."

Emma tried not to cringe. This couldn't be happening again. Every time she thought her musical career would take off and she'd land a record deal, something happened to snatch defeat out of the jaws of victory.

"I'm in the middle of preparing for a volunteer orientation today. Can we do this later, Molly?"

As in possibly never, since I don't think I'm going to like what you have to say. I definitely don't have the energy to deal with it today.

"This can't wait," Molly said. The look in her gaze only confirmed Emma's suspicions of impending doom.

As she tried to quell the unease churning in her stomach, Emma motioned for Molly to have a seat in the wooden chair on the opposite side of her less-than-impressive desk. Ah, the joys of working for a nonprofit agency. Rickety, cheap furniture.

"It's Dave, isn't it?" Emma said. Since Molly's marriage six months ago, she'd changed, showing up late for rehearsals and wanting to leave early. When she was there, she was distracted and unprepared. "He's pressuring you to leave the band, isn't he?"

She knew what that was like. *Emma, you need to grow up. Playing in a band is fine for a hobby, but it's not a real job.*

"It's not him. He's supportive of my musical career." Molly picked at the strap of the purse sitting in her lap. "It's me. I'm tired of putting my life on hold hoping for a career that's a one-in-a-million shot."

"What're you trying to say?"

"I'm leaving the band."

There was the blow Emma had been expecting, but even though she'd braced herself, it still left her reeling. All she could think was thank goodness she'd been sitting. Otherwise the news would have leveled her. Her mind scrambled to process the chaos Molly's decision created. No, she couldn't go there, refused to accept bad news until she knew she couldn't change it. "You can't quit. We're so close. I feel it. Hold off a little longer. At least until the state fair contest."

This year the Colorado state fair was having a music competition with the winner receiving a consultation with Phillip Brandise, one of the top movers and shakers in country music.

"I want to have kids. My biological clock's ticking so loud I'm going deaf. I'm afraid if I don't make some changes now I'll wake up one day and it'll be too late. I'll have given up everything that really matters, and for what? Nights spent on the stage in two-bit restaurants and bars. I've taken a job as an orchestra director at a private school in Denver, and Dave's requested a transfer. We should be able to buy a house in a few months, and hopefully soon we'll be pregnant. The movers arrive this weekend to pack everything up."

Emma stared at the other woman, someone she thought she knew fairly well, as if she'd said she was going to take up brain surgery. "How can you give up now?"

"I've found something I want more. I'll still have music in my life. It just won't be the center of my universe."

Now that Emma's shock had subsided, her anger kicked in. How dare Molly bail on the rest of the band? People who had counted on her, who thought they'd shared the same goal. "We've got appearances scheduled and the state fair is less than a month away. What're we supposed to do? Do you know how long it will take to find a replacement?"

"I meant to talk to you when I applied for the teaching position, but the time never seemed right."

"Really? I seem to remember a lot of opportunities that would've been perfect. How about when we talked about signing up for the state fair contest, or when we were planning career strategies for next year to increase our visibility and presence on social media? Those would've been pretty good times to mention you were thinking about quitting."

Molly nodded and clasped her hands in her lap. "You're right. The truth is I didn't want to face you. I didn't think you'd understand."

She was right about that. Emma didn't understand how someone could let go of a dream she'd spent years working toward, especially when they were so close.

How could they find another fiddle player, integrate that person into the band and be ready for a performance at a major contest in less than a month?

She'd manage that because she had to. Sure, she enjoyed her job at the shelter, but she didn't want to spend the rest of her life as a volunteer coordinator. Music was her life. Playing the guitar, singing and writing songs wasn't what she did. It was a part of who she was, but playing in local bars and at weddings wasn't enough. She wanted more, and no way would she let this opportunity pass her by. She'd do whatever was necessary to keep her dream alive. Nothing else mattered.

"I won't lie. I don't understand how you can say teaching music to children will be enough for you, but if you think that'll make you happy, then that's what you have to do."

I just wish your decision wasn't throwing my dream into a tailspin, but if you don't want this as much as I do, then it's a good thing you're leaving.

As she watched Molly leave, Emma thought, *six months*. That's all it would take before Molly called to say she'd made a mistake leaving the band. Life could sidetrack people with dreams. Parents got sick. Keeping a roof over their heads or wanting to eat food other than ramen noodles got in the way, but ambitions like theirs never died.

She glanced at her notes for her volunteer orientation and training but couldn't focus. As day jobs went, hers as volunteer coordinator for the Estes Park animal shelter was a pretty good one. It had its perks, the biggest of which being on tough days like today she could hide in the kennels and play with puppies until she could face the world. Yup. A little puppy therapy was the only thing that kept her going today.

Twenty minutes later Emma looked up from her spot on the kennel floor when her best friend and boss, Avery Montgomery, walked in. "You're playing with puppies. What's wrong?"

"Some days it doesn't pay to get out of bed unless you cuddle puppies." Emma pulled the wiggling black bundle closer to her chest as she gave Avery a quick rundown of her conversation with Molly. "Unless we find a new fiddle player, last weekend's performance may have been Maroon Peak Pass's swan song."

"What're the chances you can find a replacement relatively quickly?" Avery asked as she settled onto the floor beside Emma. One fluffy, roly-poly pup crawled off Emma's lap and waddled over to her friend.

"It's harder than you think. Talented musicians who are serious about their craft are already in bands and most aren't looking to change."

"Can you go on without a fiddle if you can't find someone else in time for the state fair contest?"

"It's hard enough to stand out among all the country acts. Adding Molly helped define our sound. Now all of our arrangements and the new music I've written are for a band with a fiddle. I don't want to think about how long it would take to rework everything. We'd definitely have to cancel our upcoming engagements."

"I'm sorry, Em. I know how much the band means to you." Avery scooped up a pup and scratched him behind the ears.

Avery was one of the few people in her life who truly understood how her need for a career in country music drove her. Emma wished her family understood better. They couldn't grasp why she wasn't content with her job at the shelter. It was stable and provided her with a paycheck every two weeks. She could play musician on the weekends. Why did she want more? She couldn't put her need into words. She only knew she couldn't settle for less than giving a music career her best shot. Not now, when she was older and wiser than when she'd dashed off to Nashville at eighteen all full of hopes and dreams but not much common sense.

"I wish Molly had waited a little longer to quit. Even a day. I could've handled it better. Why did she have to tell me today?" Emma bit her lip and tried to ignore the ache spreading through her. "He turns seven today. Between that and Molly's bombshell, it's too much to take."

Seven years ago she gave birth to a son and watched the nurse walk out of the room to hand him to someone else to raise.

Chapter Two

Emma didn't even know her son's name.

The pain that enveloped her after she'd given him up for adoption had been overwhelming. Looking back she had no idea how she'd gotten through those first few months, but somehow she had. While the sting had lessened over the years, her emotions still flared up at times. Certain days were worse than others—Christmas, Mother's Day and her son's birthday. Each year they became easier to get through, but something was different with his birthday this year.

"I'm sorry, Em. I forgot what today was. I can't imagine how tough this is for you every year."

"I think of him a lot, but I've been doing that more than usual lately. Sometimes I wonder what he looks like and what he's doing. Does he like sports? Is he taking piano lessons?" The list of questions was endless. Did he have her dark coloring and green eyes, or Tucker's golden hair and brown eyes? Had he inherited their musical ability?

The puppy she held snuggled closer to her chest all warm and fuzzy, full of endless energy and unconditional love. While puppy kisses couldn't fix all the world's problems, they definitely helped. "The questions

I understand, but it shouldn't hurt this much. It didn't last year. I don't get what's going on."

"Have you contacted—" Avery paused for a minute, lines of concern evident on her beautiful face.

Emma recognized the awkwardness. It showed up whenever anyone considered saying a certain phrase to her.

"It's okay. You can say the word. *Parents*. Have I contacted his parents?"

"Have you? Maybe they've changed their minds about the closed adoption. Could be they'd agree to send you photos or updates on how he's doing. Then you wouldn't have to wonder."

"You know me. I'm an all-or-nothing kind of girl. When I quit dating a guy I can't be friends. How could I be happy with emails and a few pictures?"

"I wish I had an answer for you."

Emma did, too. It would be so much easier if life came with an instruction manual. Then, during the rough spots, she could flip the book open and read the directions. For this type of life problem, do A, then B and everything will turn out great.

"I bet Tucker never thinks about me or our son." He'd barely thought about her when they were living together. The familiar anger welled up inside her—at him for his wandering eye, and other body parts for that matter, as well as at herself for her schoolgirl foolishness. "His band with that trailer-trash Miranda Lambert imitation has a top-ten album. They're on a world tour, performing in front of thousands of people while I'm playing weddings and anniversary parties."

And working a day job to pay the bills.

She and Tucker had been high school sweethearts and the star vocalists in the choir. The fall after gradu-

ation they'd packed up their belongings and headed for
Nashville. Soon after arriving, Emma had discovered
there were hundreds of other young hopefuls who'd
done the same thing, and breaking into the industry
was tougher than they imagined.

Her relationship with Tucker hadn't gone accord-
ing to plan, either. Things grew rocky between them
within a week and got steadily worse. Then, two days
after she'd told him she was pregnant, he'd waltzed
into their dumpy studio apartment and announced he
didn't love her anymore. Just like that. No buildup. No
preparation. No warning. Since by that point she wasn't
all that crazy about him either, it was a horrible relief
when he moved out.

"Hearing about how well his career is going has to
be tough," Avery said.

"I don't begrudge him his success—"

"You may not, but I sure do. He didn't earn it. Not
when the song that got him noticed and led to his recording contract was yours, too."

"I've changed my mind. You're right. He doesn't
deserve it." When Emma had stumbled across a video
of him on YouTube, she'd discovered the ass had taken
one of the songs they'd written, though he swore he
wrote it alone, changed the lyrics slightly—emphasis
on *slightly*—and performed it with his new band. The
song's video had received over a million hits and landed
him a recording contract.

That blow had broken Emma's spirit. Skinny because her morning sickness lasted all day, broke and
depressed, she'd hit rock bottom, packed up her meager
belongings and headed home to patch up her wounds.
"How could I have fallen in love with such an ass?"

"Cut yourself some slack. You were young, and he

was your first love." Avery released her squirming pup, who bounded off and tackled one of his siblings.

Age and lack of experience explained her mistake with Tucker, but what about Clint? She couldn't say the same for him, since she'd made that blunder two years ago. How could she have missed the fact that he was nothing more than Tucker version two-point-oh?

"We need to make a Tucker voodoo doll," Avery said.

"Now, why didn't I think of that? The idea has definite possibilities."

"I wonder if he'd lose his voice if we stuck pins where his vocal chords are."

"Better yet, let's harpoon him in another more private area and hope he loses use of that little piece of equipment." That would serve him right for hooking up with every blonde who could carry a tune—even if she needed a bucket to do it—when they were together.

"That's the spirit. All guys aren't like him, you know."

Avery had always believed in love and happily ever after. Even after her high school sweetheart had left for Stanford and broken up with her via email. Then, a year ago, Reed's brother was deployed to Afghanistan and he returned to Estes Park to stay with his teenage niece. After a bumpy ride, the pair had cleared the air, fallen in love all over again and married soon after that.

"If you want to take the day off, I can handle things around here."

Emma shook her head. "Thanks, but no, thanks. I'd rather be here and stay busy. If I go home all I'll do is throw on sweatpants and crawl on the couch to eat Häagen-Dazs Chocolate Chocolate Chip ice cream while I watched *Thelma and Louise*. That's just a pathetic pity party, and I refuse to do that." Not now. Not when she'd come so far. "But you can help me make that voodoo doll."

MICK HALLIGAN STOPPED when he walked into his restaurant. For a minute he stood and surveyed what he'd built. With the Formica tables, industrial-style chairs with the plastic padded seats and the country memorabilia, some people would call his place a hick bar, but looks were deceiving. His restaurant was so much more. People came to Halligan's to connect, to celebrate special times with family and friends. Everyone, staff and customers, knew each other and their lives were interconnected. They meant something to each other.

"I've got a plan, but I need your help," Mick said to his friend of almost fifty years and fellow Vietnam War vet, Gene Donovan, when he walked into the kitchen.

"Is it something for the business?" Gene asked as he stood chopping onions for the marinara sauce for the meatball sub sandwiches.

"This has to do with family. Mine and yours."

"You know whatever it is, I'm in."

"I knew you would be, but I thought I'd ask anyway."

Mick sometimes wondered how he would've made it through the hell of Vietnam if Gene hadn't been there in the trenches with him. They'd kept each other sane through the madness. Then, when shrapnel had torn Mick apart and he'd lain in a heap bleeding like a stuck pig, Gene had literally saved his life. Risking his own neck under heavy gunfire, Gene had made his way to Mick and dragged him to safety.

"I've been thinking about what matters in my life. It's family, friends, my ranch and this place. What good is having land and a business if I don't have anyone to leave them to?"

"You've got your daughter."

A daughter who'd written him off along with the rest of her past. Having a cowboy, Vietnam vet father who ran a country-western bar didn't sit well with Kimberly or her hotshot corporate executive husband.

"Fat lot of good that does me." When he'd realized Kimberly wouldn't visit him for fear of her husband learning about her wild-child past and the son she'd given up for adoption, Mick had offered to come to California, but she always had an excuse why that wouldn't work. They were moving or remodeling the house. Her husband was in the middle of a big deal at work. While he wasn't the sharpest tool in the shed, Mick had finally got the message and stopped asking.

"If I leave everything to Kimberly, all she'll do is sell what I've built and pocket the money. I'm not about to spend eternity rolling over in my grave because a developer built condos or a resort on my land, and I don't even want to think about what she'd do to this place."

Gene nodded in agreement. "That would make for an unhappy afterlife. What do you have in mind to do about it?"

"I've been thinking about Jamie. He understands the way I feel about the land and this place." Mick smiled at the memories and the wonder in his grandson's eyes when they'd ridden around the ranch for the first time. The kid had taken to being on a horse like he'd been on one all his life. Some things were just in a man's blood, and Mick knew the land was in Jamie's. "I want to leave everything to him."

"Then do it."

"I intend to, but I miss having family around. I miss

Jamie. He's my only grandchild. Hell, my only real family other than you." Since his wife, Carol, had died five years ago, the loneliness had settled into Mick's bones and his soul.

Mick glanced at the clock on the wall. The other staff wouldn't arrive for at least a half hour. Good. He didn't want anyone overhearing what he was about to say to his old friend. "I'm going to tell you something, but you've got to promise not to tell anyone."

"Haven't I kept more than one of your secrets over the years?"

"You sure have, but this one's different. It's not my secret."

Gene glared at him. "Like that makes a difference to me."

"Jamie's hand didn't heal right." Mick explained about his grandson's troubles. "I keep thinking about when I had to give up music. It damn near killed me. This place, your friendship and the love of a good woman saved me."

"Are you getting to the point about the plan and needing my help anytime soon?"

"Hold your horses. I had to tell you all this before I could get to my idea," Mick said, taking his time despite his friend's good-natured ribbing. "Jamie and your Emma would be perfect for each other. Who knows what would've happened between them if he hadn't gone back to Juilliard at the end of that summer. Hell, they might even be married by now."

"That's a mighty big leap you just took. Sure, they dated, but as I remember, it wasn't anything serious."

"If you ask me, it would've gotten serious if Jamie had been planning on sticking around. You can't tell me there wasn't a spark between our grandkids. I saw it. Could be all they need now is a little nudge to get things restarted. What harm can some matchmaking do? Mothers and grandmothers have been doing it for years."

"And men have been telling them to knock it off."

"Since we can lead the horses to water but can't make them drink, what do we have to lose?"

"They could get so mad they won't speak to us," Gene said as he stirred the simmering barbeque sauce for the pulled pork sandwiches. "That's a real possibility considering how Emma feels about musicians. She rates them between politicians and lawyers."

"This is my grandson we're talking about. Emma won't find a better man than Jamie anywhere."

"That's true, but considering the way Kimberly acted when Jamie contacted her, do you think he can get past the fact that Emma gave up a child for adoption?"

Mick still couldn't believe a child of his and Carol's had acted the way their daughter had when Jamie had contacted her ten years ago. Instead of welcoming the eighteen-year-old, his daughter had told Jamie she wanted nothing to do with him and slammed the door in his face. Then she'd called Mick, who'd told her to be honest with her husband, insisting a man who'd leave her over getting pregnant at sixteen and giving the child up wasn't worth holding on to. What he'd got for his advice was a lecture about what a wonderful man his son-in-law was and a request that Mick not have any contact with Jamie, either.

He'd told his daughter straight-out that she could do what she wanted with her life, but she couldn't tell him what to do with his, and he'd set out to locate his grandson. When he'd found Jamie a few months later, he'd invited him for a visit, and Jamie had flown to Colorado for spring break.

"I can't tell you why, but I know your granddaughter and my grandson are meant to be together. You're just gonna have to trust me."

Gene shook his head. "I would like to see Emma happy with a man who'll treat her right. What do you have in mind?"

"First, I think I'll be too sick tomorrow to pick Jamie up at the airport, and you'll be too busy handling everything here at the restaurant to go."

"And I'll ask my granddaughter to help out by picking up Jamie."

"That's the first step."

THE ENTICING SMELL of tomatoes sautéing with garlic wafted through the air as Emma rushed in the kitchen door to Halligan's. Her mouth watered and her stomach growled, making her wish she hadn't punched the snooze button so many times she had to skip breakfast. Now all she could think of was how her grandfather's meatball sub would hit the spot.

After giving Grandpa G a quick kiss on his weathered cheek, she asked, "What's so important that I have to drop everything and come over here?"

While she loved her family, sometimes she wished there weren't so many of them, or that a few of them lived farther away. Both sets of grandparents, her father and three older brothers all living in one town of eight thousand people could be overwhelming. Worse yet, she couldn't catch a cold without her entire family knowing about it within an hour, and half of them calling with advice, and yet, how often had she been at family gatherings and felt completely alone?

"Mick called. He's sick, so I have to handle things around here."

"It's not anything serious, is it?"

Her grandfather shook his head. "It's just a stomach bug, but there's no way he can make the drive to Denver to pick up his grandson at the airport. He wanted me to ask if you'd help him out by picking Jamie up."

She hadn't thought about Jamie Westland in a long time. For two summers when she was in high school they'd worked together at Halligan's. They'd even dated a few times after she'd broken up with Tucker when she'd discovered he'd been two-timing her with Monica Ritz. Had that been a big red flag waving in her face, warning her of what life would be like with Tucker, or what?

But Jamie had been different. When they'd been together he'd made her feel as though she mattered, because he'd focused solely on her. They'd gone out for pizza and caught a couple of movies that summer. Nothing major, because they'd both known he'd be returning to Juilliard in the fall. Well, except for some heavy necking. What would've happened between them if he hadn't been returning to New York? If their plans hadn't been so different? Would she still have gotten back together with Tucker? She shook her head. What good did wondering do? It wasn't as if she could change the past.

"You could have asked me that on the phone, Grandpa. If you had, it would've saved me a trip over here, and I could've had breakfast."

"Why didn't you tell me you hadn't eaten?" Her grandfather strode to the refrigerator and grabbed what she recognized as the ingredients for her favorite breakfast—an omelet with spinach, mushrooms and Roma tomatoes.

"Feeding me won't get you what you want. I can't pick Jamie up at the airport. I've got a volunteer orientation and training all day."

"That's not a problem. His flight doesn't get in until eight tonight," Grandpa G said as he threw together her omelet and poured the egg mixture into a hot pan.

So much for the convenient excuse. "Can't Jamie rent a car?"

"He's from New York City. Who knows if he can drive?"

There were people in the U.S. who couldn't drive? Really? She found that hard to believe. She thought about the summer she and Jamie had dated. "Wait a minute. I remember him driving Mick's truck on a couple of our dates."

"Oh, well. Hmm. I forgot about that." Her grandfather shuffled back and forth, his brows furrowed together in thought as he concentrated on the pan in front of him. Then he plated her omelet and handed the mouthwatering goodness to her along with a fork. "Of course, that was before he spent all those years in the Big Apple. Who knows if he still has a valid driver's license?"

"You can't be serious." She scooped up a bite of her omelet. The fluffy concoction melted in her mouth. No matter how many times she tried, hers never turned out like Grandpa G's, but she wouldn't let his wonderful cooking sway her.

"All I know is that Mick asked me to ask you to pick up Jamie at the airport, and that's what I'm doing. I don't know why you're being so difficult."

She was being difficult? She didn't know what alien had taken over her grandfather's body, but there was no reasoning with him today. "With as much family as we have in town there has to be someone else who can pick him up."

Grandpa G placed the knife on the cutting board, turned and stared at her. He waved his hand around the kitchen. "Does it look like I have time to call around to find someone else to do this for me?"

Line cooks, dishwashers and everyone else in the kitchen froze, turned and stared with their mouths hanging open in disbelief at her grandfather's sharp tone.

Now she knew something was wrong. Either that or he'd taken cranky pills along with his vitamins this morning. In her entire life she never remembered him raising his voice to anyone. She stepped around the counter and placed her hand on his arm. "What's really going on?"

He rubbed the back of his neck, and when he met her gaze, weariness filled his usually bright eyes. "I'm nervous about handling everything around here with Mick out today."

Things were growing stranger by the minute. Her grandfather routinely managed the restaurant when Mick was gone without breaking a sweat. He'd once told her that after a tour in Vietnam, he'd handled the worst life had to throw at him and nothing else could ever come close.

"Are you sure that's all that's bothering you?"

"Emma Jean, with a *J,* unlike my name, Gene with a *G,* Donovan. Do this little favor for me. Pick Jamie up at the airport. Then I won't have to worry about it."

How could she say no to that, especially after he'd pulled out the big guns by making her favorite breakfast and using her full name, emphasizing the fact that she'd been named after him? The question was why was this so important? Instinct told her she wasn't getting the whole story.

"I'll make a deal," she conceded. "I'll call around. If I can't find someone else to pick Jamie up, I will."

Her grandfather yanked the towel off his apron and swiped the cloth almost frantically across the counter, clearing away the remnants of mushrooms and spinach he'd chopped for her omelet. "You promise you'll pick Jamie up if no one else can?"

She nodded, and his rigid stance relaxed. "I heard about Molly quitting the band. Are you having any luck finding a replacement?"

The abrupt change in conversation left her a little dizzy. While he supported her musical career more than most of her family, she could count the number of times on one hand her grandfather had asked about the business side of things. "I've got some possibilities, but I've been so busy with my day job I haven't had time to contact anyone."

Luke, her bass player, had offered to make the calls, but Emma had gently nixed the suggestion. She'd put Maroon Peak Pass together. She managed their engagements, wrote their music and created their arrangements of other artists' songs. No way was anyone being scheduled to audition without her screening him first.

"You know Jamie's a fiddle player," her grandfather said. "What about asking him to play with you?"

"There's a big difference between playing in a country band and performing with a symphony. Asking Jamie to join Maroon Peak Pass would be like asking a soccer player to all of a sudden play football." As if Jamie would be interested anyway. Had her grandfather lost his mind?

"Soccer players often become kickers in football."

Vitamins. Check. Cranky pills. Check. Add taking crazy pills to the list.

"I was just throwing the idea out there."

"That's something to consider." But only if it was between canceling the band's upcoming engagements, asking Jamie or recruiting someone from the high school orchestra.

LATER THAT NIGHT Emma arrived at the Denver airport only to discover Jamie's flight had been delayed by bad weather. She'd tried to find someone else to pick him up, but she should've known how that plan would turn out and saved the time she'd wasted. Why was it whenever she needed help everyone in her family had a ready excuse? Brandon had to work at the fire station, but he was the only one with a valid reason. Everyone else either had plans like getting together with friends, or worse, they hadn't bothered to return her call.

At least she'd brought her tablet so she could work while she waited. As she sat in the unyielding chairs in the baggage claim area, she put out word on social media about the band's situation. That done, she contacted the electric fiddle players she'd thought of, managing to coerce two to audition. She called the people Luke and Grayson, their drummer, had recommended, screened them and set up auditions for a couple, despite the fact that none of the candidates seemed overly promising. The kids in the high school orchestra were looking better all the time. Lord, desperation was ugly.

The grind of the baggage claim broke into her thoughts, and she gazed at the monitor above the carousel, noting Jamie's flight had arrived.

She scanned the rush of passengers streaming into the baggage claim area. Picking Jamie out of the crowd would have been easy even if he hadn't been carrying the violin case. In the years since she'd seen him, his resemblance to Mick had become more pronounced. Same whiskey-colored straight hair, strong jaw, stark cheekbones and five-o'clock shadow. Normally she didn't like the scruffy look on men, but on Jamie, it worked. Very well.

His long, lean build had filled out and his shoulders were broader now. He'd changed from a teenager to a man. When he moved toward her, her pulse jumped and the tiniest warm glow spread through her. For a city boy, he sure had Mick's Western swagger down. Who'd have guessed that was genetic?

As she approached, his gaze zeroed in on her with an intensity that left her almost weak. She didn't know what had happened in the years since she'd seen him, but something had because it showed in his eyes. Good looks she could ignore because a pretty face could disguise a multitude of flaws, but eyes like Jamie's? That was tougher to resist. She'd always been a sucker for soulful eyes.

Too bad he had such a big strike against him—being a musician. Otherwise it might be fun getting reacquainted because he was one fine-looking man. But Emma knew better than to press her luck. For Jamie Westland, as far as she was concerned, one strike and he was out.

Chapter Three

"Emma? Right?" Jamie said, his deep brown eyes filled with curiosity when she reached him. "What're you doing here? Are you meeting someone?"

"Mick didn't tell you I was picking you up? He wasn't feeling well," she said, trying to ignore her bruised feminine ego. While they hadn't seen each other in years, how could he not remember her? They weren't exactly strangers. Not that anyone would know from his reaction to seeing her today.

No woman wanted to realize she'd been so forgettable a guy she'd dated couldn't even remember her name.

"He might have left me a message, but I forgot to turn my phone back on." Jamie reached into his back pocket and pulled out his cell.

"I guess you're not one of those people who are constantly attached to the thing, then, huh?"

"Sometimes it's nice to unplug and really get away." Heaviness tinged his voice and she wondered if something more than a simple vacation brought him to Estes Park. She shoved aside her curiosity. He was a nice guy, but considering what she had going on in her life she needed a man like she needed a two-string guitar that was out of tune.

"Sure enough. I've got a missed call from Mick and

have a voice mail," he said once he turned on his phone and glanced at the screen. After he listened to the message he said, "He probably called while I was in the air."

The grumble of the baggage conveyor belt and the conversations of family and friends reuniting swirled around them, making her more aware of the awkwardness between them.

"You didn't have to drive all the way here to pick me up. I could've rented a car."

She laughed. "You should've heard the conversation I had with my grandfather about that. He wondered if you had a valid driver's license. When I reminded him that you knew how to drive, he wondered if you'd forgotten since you live in New York City."

No reaction to her reference to their past relationship. Ouch.

"He said that? Is this the same man who could recall every memory from the time he was three with uncanny clarity? That grandfather?"

"That's the one."

Not sure what else to say, they both turned their attention to the suitcases traveling past them. She wished his bags would hurry up and arrive. The next thing they'd be talking about was the weather.

"I'm sorry my flight was late. Storms rolled in just before we were scheduled to leave. Lots of lightning and driving rain."

She wanted to groan at his comment. If things between them remained this strained, it was going to be a long ride to Estes Park. Maybe he was tired from the flight and would fall asleep in the car. That would be better than talking about the weather for an hour and a half.

They both stared straight ahead as black bags of various sizes filed past their view, the only distinguishing feature being the luggage tags. Then, out of nowhere, a toddler in denim shorts, a Grandma Loves Me Because I'm Cute T-shirt and light-up tennis shoes zoomed past them, heading for the carousel.

"Hey, little man, where are you going?" Jamie scooped up the boy, who immediately tried to wiggle free as he pointed to the parade of luggage. "I know that looks like fun, but I want you to keep all your fingers. Now, where's your mom?"

While she'd been *thinking* someone should make sure the child didn't get into trouble, Jamie had acted. Emma couldn't help but stare as the exhaustion that had lined his face and filled his voice disappeared. A huge smile lit up his features and his eyes sparkled with affection as he held the toddler.

A memory of a night years ago in Nashville when Tucker had arrived to pick her up after her shift at the diner flashed in her mind. A vacationing family with two unruly young children had been seated in her section. When she'd told him she couldn't leave until they left, Tucker said he'd wait outside and mumbled something about how parents shouldn't take their kids in public if they couldn't control them.

Definitely a different attitude from the man filling her vision now. Jamie looked so comfortable and at ease. She thought about how he'd stepped in with this child. He'd always been the kind of man who did what needed to be done without a lot of fanfare, without having to be asked. He just took care of things and those around him.

As she watched the pair, the boy grabbed Jamie's nose. Eyes alight with mischief, Jamie said, "Beep." The child's eyes widened at the sound. He released Jamie's nose, only to grab it again. "Beep."

Both males erupted into giggles, and Emma's heart tightened. Her biological clock, the one she'd have sworn possessed a dead battery, kicked into gear, making her ache. First Jamie's soulful eyes and now this. She'd have to watch her step with this guy. He could make a woman forget everything but him and the life they could have together.

"Cayden? Where are you?" A woman's panicked voice cut through Emma's thoughts.

"He's over here," she called out to the slender woman who was frantically scanning the area.

"There's your mom now," Jamie said.

"Momma?" Cayden responded as he squirmed in Jamie's arms.

"I'm hanging on to you. Who knows what trouble you'll get into if I set you free. I'm not sure the world's ready for that."

"He really could've gotten hurt if you hadn't corralled him," Emma said.

"I was a lot like this guy when I was young. Sometimes I had more curiosity than common sense." He peered down at the boy in his arms. "Pal, you're gonna have to work on curbing that before it gets you into major trouble."

"You're right about that," Cayden's mother said when she reached them. She tucked stray strands of hair that had come loose from her sloppy ponytail behind her ear before she took her son from Jamie and introduced herself. She then hugged the boy so tight he squealed in protest. "I can't thank you enough for snagging him. My friend was supposed to meet us, but she must be running late. We've been in New York visiting my parents. I turned around to grab my suitcase and Cayden was gone. I've never been so scared in my life."

"Glad I could help, Dana," Jamie said.

"Do you need a ride? Are you sure your friend's coming?" Emma asked.

Before Dana could answer, her cell phone pinged. "I bet that's her now." She dug through the diaper bag, located her phone and checked her texts. After discovering her friend was waiting outside the airport, she thanked Jamie again, and then before she left, she leaned over to whisper in Emma's ear. "He's going to make a great father. Don't let him get away. There aren't a lot like him left these days."

Even if Emma was looking for someone to spend the rest of her life with, she wouldn't chose a musician. They were too temperamental and the business was too demanding. Making it and staying anywhere close to the top took everything a person had to give and still the business wanted more. Two people with those kinds of pressures couldn't maintain a relationship.

Too bad because unless he'd changed a lot, Dana was right. Jamie still looked like one of the good guys.

EMMA DONOVAN. JAMIE had almost stopped cold when he saw her in the baggage claim at the airport. How he'd managed to act nonchalant, even going so far as to pretend he didn't remember her name, he didn't know. Especially when his heart had been banging against his ribs like cymbals during a John Philip Sousa march.

Slender, yet curvy enough to fill a man's hands, she'd filled out in all the right ways and looked even better than she had in high school. With her long black hair and shining green eyes, Emma sure could get his pulse going. He remembered her all too well…and the fact that he'd been more interested in her than she'd been in him when they'd dated. She'd been seventeen and he nineteen. When he'd heard she'd broken up with her boyfriend, he'd jumped at the chance to ask her out. They'd gone out a few times, and then she'd ended things with him. Emma had taught him a valuable lesson: never be the first guy a woman dates after breaking up with her boyfriend. In this case, being number one was not what a guy wanted.

"When did you move back to town?" he asked in a lame attempt at conversation as they made their way to the parking lot and her car.

"It's been almost two years."

"Mick said you were in Nashville singing with a band, and that things were going well. What brought you back?"

"This and that." She unlocked the doors and got in her car. The door closed with a quiet thud behind her. "How about you? What brings you to Estes Park?"

Her short comment, combined with how she gripped the steering wheel so tight her fingers whitened, sent a message even a guy with the social skills of a Neanderthal could read. He'd touched on a sore subject.

"Doesn't the Philharmonic have a tour coming up? Mick's been telling anyone who would listen all about it. I'm surprised you could get away."

Now he cringed. Discussions about his career and its impending doom were exactly what he'd come to get away from, but what did he expect? When people hadn't seen each other for years or just met, what did they ask about? A person's career. What could he say that was the truth, yet wasn't, and didn't lead to any further discussion?

"They didn't have a problem with me leaving." He tried not to wince at what he'd said, since technically

it was true. He was just leaving out the more important details.

He stared out the window as they left the airport
parking lot and turned onto Interstate 270 West. As
the Denver city lights faded into the distance, the sun
turned the rugged Rocky Mountains all orange and yel-
low. The beauty of the land still amazed Jamie. The
constant strength of the mountains tapped into a part
of him that craved stability and certainty. The Rockies
would always be here. He liked that. They gave him
something to come back to again and again.

"It's been raining a lot in New York lately," he said
when he couldn't stand the silence any longer. "I'm glad
to be getting away from that. Hopefully the weather
will stay nice so I can do some hiking and horseback
riding while I'm here."

"If the weather forecasters are right, you should be
fine."

It was going to be a long hour and a half to Estes
Park. They could only talk about the weather for so
long.

WHEN EMMA TURNED onto the drive leading to Mick's
house, Jamie thanked her again for the ride. "I'm sure
I'll see you around."

"In a small town it's hard not to."

Don't sound so excited. More disappointment than he
wanted to admit spun through him. *Message received.*
He opened the car door, grabbed his suitcase and headed
up the walkway to Mick's house as Emma drove away.
Too bad, though. They could have had some fun, and
he could use a little of that right now.

Mick sat waiting for him, perched in his rocking

chair on the front porch. "So life's been a little rough lately."

"It could be better, but then I guess it could be worse." And would be if his hand failed to regain its strength and dexterity.

His grandfather nodded toward the front door. "You know the way to your room. Drop your stuff off and meet me back here. I swear there's no better place to think than this front porch."

As Jamie walked into the house, he smiled at the pictures of Mick when he'd played with his band, ones of his life with his wife and events at Halligan's displayed everywhere. The progression of a life. One that meant something. Like his parents' house, this place was a home filled with memories where love lingered in every corner.

Once upstairs in the spare bedroom, he placed his suitcase in the corner. Nothing about this room had changed since the first night he'd slept here. The antique furniture so like Mick himself—Western in style, strong, sturdy and able to stand the test of time—had belonged to Mick's parents, a tangible link to past ancestors. He ran his hand over the quilt his grandmother had made, wishing he'd had more time to get to know her.

Once back on the porch, he sank into the weathered rocking chair Mick had given his wife when they'd moved into the house as newlyweds, and he stared at the mountains looming around him.

"Emma really helped me out, but then, that's what she does. She's a good girl, that one. She's held her family together over the past two years."

Was that what had stolen the sparkle he used to see

in her eyes? She'd seemed different from what he remembered. Subdued. Distant almost.

"She needs to have a life of her own, but every time she tries to, something happens," Mick added, and glanced his way as if expecting him to ask for details.

The words to ask what had happened with Emma sat perched on Jamie's tongue, but he pushed aside the thought. He had enough on his mind without looking for more.

"Now her fiddle player's quit."

"That's too bad," Jamie said, refusing to rise to the bait Mick dangled in front of him. He was here to clear his head and sort out his future. Women had a way of short-circuiting a man's brain. Best to keep from sticking his nose in where it didn't belong. A lot safer, too.

The moon cast a pale glow over the mountains. Gazing over land that had been in Mick's family for generations, Jamie couldn't help but feel a connection to his past. At times he felt like two people compressed into one body. The person created by his DNA that determined his height, the color of his eyes and his musical ability, and the person created by the parents who'd raised him. But what percentage came from which source? He suspected his need for stability, his craving an anchor in his life came from his parents. They'd provided that calm presence, that guiding force in his life, and the older he got the more he wanted that same connection they had with each other. The one he saw flicker in their eyes when they smiled at each other.

He wasn't sure how long he and Mick sat rocking on the porch. The rustling wind through the trees mixed with the creaking of the rockers and their voices as they talked about the restaurant, the ranch and what Jamie could do to keep busy. The conversation soothed his battered nerves. Nothing important or earth-shattering, but the chat was exactly what he needed. Ordinary and uncomplicated.

"I haven't told anyone about your hand, so no one should bother you about that here, but I am going to say one thing about what you're going through. Then I won't bring it up again," Mick said. "Just because you can't play the fiddle like you used to doesn't mean you can't play another instrument. Maybe you could play guitar in a country band. You ever thought about that?"

Jamie shook his head. "I never considered doing anything else." Probably because he hadn't been exposed to other types of music growing up. When his musical ability became apparent, his parents had encouraged him to pursue classical music. That's what they listened to. Math and music went hand in hand. Classical music appealed to them because it possessed a sense of order, precision and structure. Contemporary music seemed so chaotic to them.

"I think you'd be a natural," Mick continued. "After all, you're my grandson, and it's clear you got my musical talent."

As an adult, when he listened to music he chose country or rock. Listening to classical felt too much like work. Popular music let him escape. But playing it? He mulled the idea over. Maybe Mick's suggestion wasn't that crazy. Something new might be just what he needed. For as long as he could remember he'd sung around the house and made up tunes. He smiled recalling how that habit used to drive his sisters crazy. At five he'd started composing his own songs and performing for the family.

"That's something to consider."

Because if he couldn't return to the symphony, he

couldn't see his life without performing. Not that teaching wasn't a worthy profession, but there was something about being onstage that gave him a high as addictive as any drug, left him aching for a fix now, but it was more than that. He knew performing was where he was meant to be.

"Which hand do you use on the neck of that fancy fiddle of yours?"

"The left. The one I injured." If he'd injured his bow hand he might have been able to stay with the symphony.

"String instruments have a lot in common," Mick said. "With a guitar you play the chords with your left hand. That doesn't take as much dexterity. You do all the fast picking and strumming with your right hand. The hand that's working just fine."

Mick stood, headed into the house and returned a minute later with a guitar, which he handed to Jamie. "This was my first guitar. When I was a teenager I took any job I could get to save up to buy this. After I got hurt I couldn't bring myself to give it away. I guess part of me never quit hoping I'd be able to play again."

The instrument felt awkward in Jamie's grasp, almost backward as he settled the guitar on his lap. He wrapped his left hand around the neck. He rested his other hand against the smooth wood. His fingers itched to strum across the strings.

Jamie mulled over the idea, not sure how he felt about picking up another instrument. A little voice in his head urged him to think of the guitar as another way to work his hand. Movement was exercise, and that couldn't hurt. Combine playing the guitar with some good old-fashioned hard work and practicing his violin…who knew what could happen? All he wanted was his life back, any way he could get there.

"Can you show me how to play a couple of chords?"

THE NEXT AFTERNOON Jamie stood behind the bar at Halligan's unloading the dishwasher and checking stock. The physical work around the restaurant felt good. He'd been in Colorado for less than twenty-four hours, but he already felt different, almost as though he'd left his problems behind in New York. 'Course it helped that no one here was asking him what he was going to do or looking at him as if his life was over and he'd disintegrate before their eyes.

As he iced down bottles of beer for the dinner crowd, his gaze strayed to Emma, who'd shown up with her band a while ago to audition violinists. Her arrival had definitely improved the view and brightened his day. Tall enough that a man wouldn't get a stiff neck having to bend down to look at her, Emma wasn't so tall she looked him in the eye. Her jeans molded to her feminine curves. Her black hair spilled over her shoulders.

While he hadn't spent the past several years mooning over her, he admitted she'd crept into his thoughts more than a time or six, and not just because of her looks, though she could make any man stop and look twice in her direction. Something else pulled him to her. Her openness, the warmth in her shining green eyes and her smile grabbed his attention more than anything else.

When she and the band launched into another song with their current candidate, her voice, belting out the haunting melody, echoed through the room. Angels would be tempted to trade their wings to sing like Emma. Plus she played guitar like a master. The sound she drew out of her instrument could fill a man with joy or make him weep depending on her whim. He stopped dead in his tracks to listen and enjoy. The music swirled around him, working its way inside, seducing him.

While Emma's skills impressed him, he couldn't say the same about the violinists. Noting the slight frown on Emma's face and how her brows knitted together, he suspected she agreed. When this latest candidate sang harmony on the chorus, he wasn't bad, but something was off. The notes were all there, but their voices didn't mesh. Like chocolate and steak. Both good things, but together? No, thanks. But more important, Emma overpowered the man's voice even though Jamie sensed she was backing off.

When the song ended a minute later, she thanked the man and told him they'd let him know when they made a decision. Even from across the room, Jamie could see the guy realized it was a no-go. A person either felt the connection and the music worked in a group or it didn't. This combination clearly didn't. Jamie couldn't blame the guy for being disappointed, though. Who wouldn't wake up raring to race into work if he found Emma waiting for him?

As the musician packed up his instrument, Emma strolled toward the bar and almost collapsed on a stool. "I always thought auditions were bad from the auditioning point of view. Now I'm realizing they're not so hot from the other side, either." She reached into her jeans pocket and slapped a five onto the bar. "I desperately need a Diet Coke. The ibuprofen didn't work, but maybe the caffeine will keep my headache from going nuclear."

"I'm still in training, but I think I can handle that. Want me to put some rum in it? You look like you could use it." Then he cringed. Slick move. Tell a girl she looks worn out. "That didn't come out right."

"I should be offended at the comment and fire off a snappy comeback to put you in your place, but I'll have to give you a rain check. The auditions have left me brain-dead." She massaged her temples. "Add the rum. After all, it's five o'clock somewhere, and we have two more auditions. I can use the liquid courage."

"Do you always practice here?"

She shook her head. "Normally we use my dad's garage, but the acoustics are better here, and for the auditions I wanted to get a better sense of how someone moves onstage. The garage is a little cramped for that."

"Your band's good. Your voice and guitar skills are phenomenal. What're you doing playing local joints like this?"

When pain flashed in her eyes, he wanted to snatch the question back. Boy, he was on a roll. How could he have forgotten she'd made it clear yesterday that she didn't want to discuss her career or what had brought her back to Estes Park? Now he'd done just that. So much for having better social skills than a Neanderthal.

"I ask myself that daily. Every time I think I've got a shot at making it big, something happens."

"Like someone leaves the band." At her raised eyebrows, he added, "Mick mentioned your violinist quit."

"If it's not something like that, then it's life getting in the way."

The defeat in her voice tugged at him, making him want to ease whatever weighed on her. *Get over it. You've got enough piled on your plate without sneaking a bite off someone else's.*

He reached for a glass on the shelf. When he moved to place it on the plastic mat behind the bar, his hand cramped. The glass slipped from his grasp, hit the cement floor and shattered.

Applause erupted from the staff. After executing an exaggerated bow, he said, "Let me try that again with a little more skill." He tried to ignore the twitches in his left hand as he reached for a glass with his right. After he fixed Emma's drink without mishap and placed it in front of her, he grabbed the small hand broom and dustpan and cleaned up his mess.

"Don't tell Mick you broke a glass. He'll take it out of your pay," she teased.

That was the least of his worries. "Since I'm working for room and board, I'll have to go to bed without dinner and sleep in the barn." Then, wanting to get the conversation on a safer topic, he said, "I hope the last two guys you've got lined up are better. The people you've auditioned so far don't match the rest of the band's ability. The first guy has possibilities. He had a tendency to drag at the beginning, but he resolved the problem quickly. Could be he'd get over that issue once he learned your style."

"Thanks for confirming my opinion, but even if he fixes the tempo issues, I'm not sure he's right for us. Technically he's fine, but he lacks something. He's almost wooden. There's no spark in his eyes or his voice when he sings."

"I noticed that, too. Could be he was nervous. Is he in a band now?" She nodded. "How's he look when he's onstage with them?"

"Like he's got a broom handle tied to his back."

"Chances are that won't change."

"That's what I'm afraid of." She sipped her drink. "We haven't performed without a fiddle in over a year. If we don't find someone soon we'll have to overhaul our repertoire or cancel appearances."

"That's rough. If my mom were here, she'd say the

most complicated problems can bring the most powerful opportunities."

"She sounds like a wise woman. I'll try to remember that."

The front door to the restaurant opened, drawing their attention. A thirtysomething man held the door, his face beaming brighter than the sunshine spilling in behind him as he gazed at his wife and the swaddled baby she cradled in her arms.

"Sorry, folks. We aren't open yet."

"Nonsense. Come on in." Emma turned to Jamie. "Mick won't mind."

Jamie eyed her. "Is that true, or are you saying that because you enjoy contradicting me?"

"There is that, but in this case it's true. Matt and Naomi are regulars."

"You say that like there are people in town who aren't."

"Good comeback." She waved the couple forward. For the first time, the light he remembered twinkled in her eyes, making her face shine. "Don't mind Jamie. Have a seat so I can see the baby. I was thrilled for you when I heard the news."

"We never thought this day would come," Naomi said as she and her husband walked toward the bar. "We had to wait quite a while, but she was worth it."

Emma peered down at the baby. "She's beautiful. What's her name?"

"Lillian Rose."

"We named her after our grandmothers," Matt added.

Emma asked about all the important statistics like when she was born, her weight and length. As Naomi answered the questions, she rubbed her daughter's smooth cheek. "We were in the delivery room with the birth mother, and got to see Lily come into this world. That was such an incredible moment. Were the adoptive parents there with you when your baby was born?"

Jamie froze. An iron fist clenched his stomach. *Were the adoptive parents there with you when your baby was born?* Emma had given birth to a child and given it up for adoption? When had that happened? He caught sight of her out of the corner of his vision. What did he expect? That he'd somehow be able to tell she'd given birth? Then he stole a look at her face. Was she a little pale? Her even teeth nibbled on her lower lip as if she struggled to keep her emotions under control.

Could seeing this couple's excitement be tough for her? Maybe not all women who gave up a child had a heart of stone like the woman who'd given birth to him.

Chapter Four

Emma saw Jamie's eyes widen and his facial features tighten, revealing tiny lines around his eyes. *He didn't know.*

She was so accustomed to small-town life where everyone knew everything about her, it never occurred to her he might not know she'd given a child up for adoption. She could almost see the gears turning in his head as he struggled to process the information. *He's reevaluating everything he thought he knew about me.* Shutting out his reaction, she turned to the couple beside her.

"The adoptive parents were at the hospital, but not in the delivery room with me. We had a closed adoption."

Naomi nodded in understanding. "It was a wonderful bonding experience. Matt got to cut the umbilical cord. We feel so honored that our birth mother chose us."

Life could be so backward. Teenagers who lacked the good sense to keep a houseplant alive got pregnant when their boyfriends dropped their pants, but couples like the Sandbergs couldn't conceive. "You two will be wonderful parents."

"We're going to do our best." Naomi reached out and placed her delicate hand on Emma's arm. "I hope seeing us doesn't bring up too many painful memories for you."

None that she couldn't handle. "It's great getting to see how excited you are. I did what was best for my child. He's much better off being raised by two loving parents. Seeing you with Lily only reinforces that." Emma twirled the straw in her drink, swirling the ice, which clinked against the glass. "It's nice seeing the joyful side of adoption. Thanks for giving me that."

Naomi wiped her eyes. "We're here to meet with Mick about the family get-together we're having so everyone can meet Lily. We want him to cater the party."

"I'll find him for you." Jamie glanced at Emma, concern in his warm gaze, as if to ask permission. As if he were worried about her. How odd was that? She flashed him what she hoped passed for an I'm-fine smile and not one that revealed how off balance she felt. After he left for the kitchen, she congratulated Naomi and Matt again and said she needed to rejoin the band for the auditions. As she walked toward the stage on legs she worried would collapse under her, she glanced at her watch, noting she had twenty minutes until the next audition. When she reached her bandmates, she said, "How about we take a break? I need some fresh air to clear my head."

She needed time to fall apart, give in to her pity over what might have been and put herself back together.

Both men nodded. She saw the questions in their eyes, but they said nothing. For a minute, as she walked toward Halligan's back door, the fact that her bandmates failed to comment on how she wasn't quite herself stung. But what did she expect? When she'd formed Maroon Peak Pass they'd discussed keeping their personal lives and their work separate. No getting chummy, going out to dinner or socializing at each other's houses. No sticking their noses into each other's affairs. She'd made the mistake of blurring the lines before with disastrous results. When she'd laid out her expectations she'd explained that, in her experience, all that led to were messy disagreements, hurt feelings and band breakups. Considering what she'd said, she had no right to be disappointed when the guys gave her exactly what she'd asked for, and yet she was.

Once in the alley she collapsed on a wooden crate near the wall, and the tears spilled down her cheeks. She appreciated seeing the happier side of adoption, but the encounter with Naomi and Matt still dredged up memories she'd rather keep buried. More than it should. Her emotions regarding the adoption hadn't been this raw in years. She shouldn't be sitting here falling apart and feeling as if she'd been run over by a truck when she'd made the right decision.

The back door creaked open, and Emma swiped a hand across her eyes. The lie that she'd come out to get fresh air and the wind blew something into her eye perched on her tongue—she turned expecting to see someone bringing out the garbage or sneaking out for a smoke. Instead there stood Jamie, concern radiating from his gaze.

Those eyes could hypnotize a girl or make her spill every secret she held close.

"You okay?" He shoved his hands in his pockets. "I was concerned when the guys were onstage, but you weren't."

"I'm fine and dandy." She flashed him her best I'm-pretending-I'm-on-top-of-the-world smile. "I'm gathering my courage for the next audition."

She stared him down, and suspected he was trying to decide whether or not to call her bluff. *Come on, fold.*

"Your eyes give you away." He stepped closer. When

he stood in front of her, his hand cupped her face and his thumb brushed across her skin. "There's a tear on your cheek."

She closed her eyes, savoring his touch. The simple comfort of it. It would be so easy to step into his arms, to find reassurance and strength there, and his concerned gaze told her he was more than willing to offer those things.

Instead she leaned away from him and crossed her arms over her chest. She couldn't do this; she refused to feel anything for him. She had her goals. Her plan mapped out. Nothing would get in her way. Least of all, a man.

He nodded toward the door. "That had to be rough for you. I never knew you gave up a child for adoption."

She nodded. "He turned seven this week."

As Jamie sank onto the wooden crate beside her, she could tell he was doing the math in his head. "What were you? Eighteen or nineteen when you had him?"

She nodded, and shoved the memories into the back of her mind before they bubbled over again. "Deciding to give him up for adoption was the hardest thing I've ever done. I knew there was happiness and joy, the thrill of the new life ahead of them as a family on the other side, but I never *saw* it until today. It wasn't real."

"Seeing you in there hit home for me how hard the decision could be for the birth mother."

So they'd both learned something. "Rumor around town said when you first contacted Kimberly, it didn't go well."

He chuckled, she sensed more out of nervousness than humor. "That's an understatement. The *Titanic*'s voyage went smoother."

"I'm sorry."

"It hurt at first, but finding out she doesn't have much to do with Mick, either, helped. I realize now it's not my problem. It's hers." He leaned toward her. "Despite knowing that, every once in a while something happens, and I get kicked in the teeth. Kind of like you did today."

He understood in a way no one else could. "It's been weird the past couple of weeks. My son's been on my mind more lately. I've got this funny feeling. I can't put it into words, but it's almost like I'm worried something's wrong."

"Contact his parents."

For the first time since she'd given up her child, a person failed to stumble over the phrase.

"Closed adoption, remember?"

"Circumstances change. Deals get renegotiated all the time."

"I agreed to that condition for good reasons, and those haven't changed. Coping with a birth mom as an adult has to be hard enough. You discovered that. But as a seven-year-old? I don't want this being about me and what I need. It has to be about what's best for my son."

"It takes a helluva person to realize that."

She clasped her hands in her lap to keep from picking at her nail polish. "I'm not sure being involved with him is what's best for me, either. Would it be like trying to eat half a cookie? I've never been good at moderation."

"So you'd work on the issue, get better at it."

Life had a way of throwing enough hardships that could land a kid on a therapist's couch without her tossing stuff at her son. That's what worried her most. "How old were you when you found out you were adopted?"

"I was in third grade. We were studying probability in school. I remember Mrs. Little talking about recessive genes and eye color. She said when two brown-eyed people have children there were three possible outcomes. She drew this table on the board to show us." His forearms braced on his thighs, he leaned forward, staring straight ahead, his gaze hooded and distant. "I asked what the probability of two blue-eyed people having a brown-eyed child was. Mrs. Little told me that couldn't happen."

"Your parents both have blue eyes?"

He nodded. "That's why I was so sure she was wrong. When I got home, I found out Mrs. Little had called my mom to tell her what happened. That's when my parents told me I was adopted."

"How would you have felt if you were seven and someone showed up saying she gave birth to you?"

"I don't know what I would've thought. At that age, all I thought was that the person that had me couldn't raise me so I got different parents."

"What about your parents? How would they have felt?"

"That's a tougher question. They were very supportive when I contacted Kimberly and Mick, but I was eighteen."

"And by then your relationship was established."

"Exactly, and I told them searching for my birth mother wouldn't change that."

"What about your birth father?"

"Kimberly isn't even sure who that is."

Now she'd really stepped in it. She tried to think of what to say, but words failed her.

"Don't feel bad about asking. It is what it is."

"I wish I knew what to do. How to shake this odd feeling I've had lately."

"At least call the parents. Explain how you've been

feeling. Tell them all you want to know is that your son's okay."

She'd never considered that option. Once she knew her son was fine, that nothing was wrong, her life could return to normal. Reminders of her child would pop up some days to throw her off stride, but then the ache would recede again. "There's one problem. Since it was a closed adoption I don't think the agency will give me any information on the parents."

"If they won't, I can help. I've gone through that kind of search."

"You'd do that?"

"Why's that so hard to believe?"

She thought about his question. Why was it so hard to believe someone would offer to help her? Probably because she wasn't the type of person everyone rushed to assist. Her family assumed she could take care of herself. After all, she'd held her own growing up with three older brothers. She came from strong stock, and that's how everyone treated her. "I appreciate the offer."

She could at least contact the agency to tell them if the adoptive parents expressed interest, she was open to exploring a relationship, as well.

A knock sounded on the door, followed by Luke poking his head outside. "Our next audition's here."

She nodded. "I'll be right there."

When the door closed again, she turned to Jamie, wanting to say something to thank him for his unexpected kindness, but she couldn't find the words. What he'd done by listening and really hearing her had helped her process what she'd been feeling.

When was the last time anyone other than Avery had really listened to her? The past two years it seemed as if when anyone called or stopped by to chat it was because they needed something. Her dad called when he ran out of meals in the freezer. Her grandparents, excluding her Grandpa G, called when they needed a prescription picked up or a ride to a doctor's appointment. Her brothers called, well, never.

But no one other than her best friend called to just talk or to see how she was doing.

Until Jamie.

Before she could change her mind, she jumped up and wrapped her arms around him for a quick hug. "Thanks for everything. For listening."

Then she darted for the door and the safety of the restaurant.

WHEN JAMIE WALKED back inside he watched Emma dash across the restaurant, his body still humming from having hers pressed up against him. His gaze locked on the sway of her hips and he smiled. Who'd have guessed cowboy boots could put the same special something into a woman's walk that high heels did? He was accustomed to women in designer jeans and expensive stilettos, but he was gaining a new appreciation for a simple pair of Wranglers and boots. They made a woman look real, accessible and damn fine.

"You ready?" Mick asked when Jamie joined him behind the bar.

"As ready as I'll ever be." Jamie pulled his gaze away from Emma. "Is there anything else we need to go over before the dinner rush hits?"

"It still gets pretty crazy in here on a weekend night, but don't worry. Usually no one's in a big hurry, especially when we've got a band. They come for dinner and to spend time with family and friends. Then they hang around to listen to music and dance." Mick nodded toward the stage. "I sure hope Emma can find someone to take Molly's place. All that girl's ever wanted to do was sing country music."

"You two gonna stand here jawin' all afternoon, or can one of you deal with the liquor delivery out back?" Gene said as he stormed out of the kitchen.

"I never should have made you day manager. You always were the power-hungry type," Mick joked.

"Fine. It's not my business that'll suffer when we run out of whiskey." Then Gene turned and headed back through the swinging double doors.

"Come on, Jamie. I'll check the order, and you can do the heavy lifting."

The rest of the afternoon went faster than Jamie expected, and then the dinner rush hit. After a couple of hours he felt as though he'd met or gotten reacquainted with all of Estes Park's eight thousand residents while manning the bar. Jamie flexed his hand, stretching out the tight muscles. He'd been amazed how much the repeated motion of picking up glasses had worked his hand, and except for the one dropped glass, he'd done well.

But his hand wasn't the only thought plaguing him tonight. His mind kept wandering back to Emma. Instead of leaving after her auditions, she joined a couple of girlfriends at a table that always managed to stay within his sight no matter how many people crowded around the bar.

As Jamie handed another patron his beer, Mick's cell phone rang. When his grandfather ended the call a few seconds later, his face lined with concern, he turned to Jamie. "That was tonight's band. Their truck broke down. They won't be here for at least an hour." Mick glanced around the crowded restaurant. "The natives are getting restless, which means they could start leaving. Which means their money walks out with them. How about you play something to settle 'em down until the band gets here?"

Jamie stared at his grandfather and thought the man had lost his mind. Had he forgotten about his hand? He leaned closer so the customers clustered around the bar wouldn't hear. "I'm not ready for that. I dropped a glass today because my hand cramped up."

"Hell, that happens to everyone."

"Even if I felt comfortable playing, my music isn't the stuff this crowd wants to hear. There would be a stampede for the door."

"Then don't play your fancy fiddle. Use the karaoke machine. You got a good voice." When Jamie opened his mouth to object, his grandfather continued, "And before you start saying you don't know how to sing any country-western songs, I heard you singing along to the Willie Nelson songs Gene played in the kitchen this afternoon. Sing one of those."

Jamie nodded toward Emma's table. "Ask Emma's band to fill in."

"I could do that, but by the time she gets a hold of everyone, they get back here and then set up, the band I scheduled should be here and half of my customers will be gone. I need someone on that stage right now."

"Hey, Mick, where's the band?" a thirtysomething man dressed in the local uniform of jeans, plaid shirt and cowboy hat asked after he ordered two more beers. "Janet and I are here to listen to some music. We got a sitter tonight and everything. Let's get this party started."

After tossing Jamie a see-I-told-you look, Mick said, "The band's running a little late. They had car trouble."

"How late is a little? If it's much longer, Janet and I may have to go to the new chain place that opened down the street. I promised her we'd go dancing."

"What? The band's not coming?" another man at the bar said.

"Hold on there. The band will be here, and I'm working on fixing the problem of having some music to tide us over." Mick patted Jamie on the back. "My grandson here's a fine musician and has a good voice to boot. He's going to get a karaoke night started. People can dance if they want, and that'll hold everyone until the band gets here."

Jamie cringed. How could he say no to that? He wiped his sweaty palms on the bar rag, tossed the cloth aside and stared at the older man beside him. "I'll do one song, and then I'm done."

Once onstage, his gaze landed on Emma. He'd pretend he was talking to her. Maybe that would help ease his nerves. "Hello, everyone. For those of you I haven't met tonight, I'm Mick's grandson, Jamie. There's been a little detour in tonight's plans. The band's truck broke down so we're going to have a karaoke night until they get here. Thanks to Mick's arm-twisting—"

"Yeah, he's good at that," someone from the crowd tossed out.

Everyone laughed and some of Jamie's tension eased. "Tell me about it. I was tending bar, and the next thing I knew I was promoted to entertainer. Promise you'll be gentle with me."

"I can show you a good time, and I promise to be gentle," a woman shouted from one of the back tables.

Jamie swallowed hard, and laughed along with everyone else. This wasn't like being on the stage at the Philharmonic. Never once had a woman in the audience hollered out that she wanted to show him a good time. What had he gotten himself into?

As EMMA SAT at a table near the stage with Avery and her friend's sister-in-law Stacy, she stared at Jamie. For someone who spent a good portion of time onstage performing with a symphony, he looked very uncomfortable. His posture was rigid and his voice as he introduced himself lacked his casual assurance. Now there was almost a brittle quality to it. While he joked and smiled at the crowd, his eyes held a look similar to those of a collie brought into the shelter after his owner died—completely confused and overwhelmed.

But then symphony crowds weren't known for shouting out what a good time they'd show a man. Something the rowdy crowd at Halligan's could be known to do at least once an hour. Especially if Carla Timmons was in the crowd and had a few margaritas in her.

"I'm sure you could show me a thing or two, but right now I'm working. I can't let my boss down," Jamie said, a tight smile on his face.

"Better cut Carla off, Mick, before she rushes the stage," someone else called out.

"Poor Jamie. Carla's in rare form tonight," Avery said. "Do you know when Jamie got into town? Have you two talked?"

"He got here yesterday," Emma said. "I picked him up at the airport when Mick wasn't feeling well."

"Why didn't you tell me?"

"There's nothing to tell." *Except Jamie looked so incredible holding this toddler at the airport yesterday my biological clock started ticking again, and then this afternoon he was so sweet when he came to make sure I was okay. A girl could get used to a guy doing stuff like that.*

No way was she sharing that info.

"You two dated for a while, didn't you?"

Emma nodded. "That summer after graduation, but it wasn't any big deal."

She glanced at the stage. Jamie shifted his stance from foot to foot, his movements stiff and awkward. Even dressed in jeans and the hunter-green Halligan's T-shirt, he looked out of place. She shook her head when she noticed his shoes. For goodness sake, the man was wearing tennis shoes. That had to be a first for this stage. How had Mick ever let him out of the house with those on?

"No big deal? That's not what I remember about you and Jamie. You two went everywhere together. You said he was a good kisser," Avery said, a big know-it-all-best-friend grin on her face.

Good enough to make my toes curl. Thanks for reminding me. That was the last thing she needed to remember right now. Emma rolled her eyes. "I don't remember that conversation, and even if it were true, what does it matter? Jamie and I aren't teenagers anymore. We've changed a lot since then."

"I bet kissing's not the only thing he's good at," Stacy said, her dreamy gaze locked on Jamie.

"Get a grip, you two. You're both married, and the way you're looking at him is embarrassing."

"We're not the only one giving him the eye." Avery nodded toward the crowd around them.

"I know. So is every female in the place."

"Including you," Stacy added.

"Let it go." Emma didn't dare deny the statement, she wasn't that accomplished a liar.

"You're awfully touchy about this subject. Are you sure nothing happened between you two when you picked him up at the airport?"

Something happened between us today, and it left me more scared than I've been in a long time. "What's with the third degree?"

"Have you thought about starting things up with him?" Avery asked, a huge silly grin on her face.

"Now I get it. This is payback for our night here when Reed first got back in town, isn't it?"

"It's not much fun being in the hot seat, is it?" Avery said. "I've got to say an interrogation is more enjoyable from this side."

"Sounds like a good story. Share," Stacy coaxed.

"Just replay this conversation, but change the names to Avery and Reed," Emma said. Hoping her friends would get the message she was done with this particular topic, Emma turned her attention to Jamie.

"Key up one of those songs Gene had on earlier," he said to his grandfather who stood offstage.

"'Always on My Mind' coming up," Mick replied.

How could Mick do this to his grandson? Jamie's awkwardness reached out to Emma. Talk about looking like a broom handle had been tied to his back. The man was a classically trained musician. Someone should rescue him. She pushed back her chair.

Then Jamie cleared his throat and turned to Mick. "Toss me your hat."

The tan cowboy hat spun through the air. Jamie caught it by the brim and put it on. Cheers and whistles sounded from the audience. "That's better."

It certainly was. Now, if he had on a good pair of Ariat boots he'd be close to perfect.

"Now I'm feeling more at home," Jamie said as the

music started. He closed his eyes for a minute and started singing.

While he stumbled over the words, the strength of his tenor voice filled the room. His stiffness faded and his features relaxed. Emma sat there as if her butt had been nailed to the chair, unable to do anything but stare, and she wasn't easy to impress. Why wasn't he singing professionally? Not sharing a magnificent singing voice like his was criminal. Even struggling with the words, he possessed an assurance. He commanded the room, but there was also something in the way he moved. A healthy dose of confidence mixed with grace and a whole lot of sensuality.

Be still my heart.

The song ended and the bar erupted in applause, but she still couldn't move.

Someone shook her arm, pulling her out of her haze. "Emma, come back to earth." When she turned, Avery leaned closer, an I-know-what-you've-been-thinking-about smirk on her face. "And you might want to close your mouth. If you don't, you're going to start drooling. Not that I blame you. That man is certainly drool-worthy."

"It has nothing to do with how he looks." Emma ignored the urge to duck under the table in case the Lord sent a lightning bolt to strike her down for her blatant lie. "I couldn't help but admire his voice. It's incredible."

Avery's bright laugh swirled around her. "And you really think I'm going to believe that's all it was?"

"I'm going to ignore that comment."

"Because you can't deny it."

"Now it's your turn," Jamie said to the crowd, thankfully drowning out the brewing second inquisition

Avery was gearing up to start. "Who wants to come up and sing next?"

Before he finished the question, Shay Edwards bounced past Emma's table and practically vaulted onto the stage. Quite a feat considering her jeans were so tight they had to be cutting off circulation to her legs. When Jamie tried to hand her the microphone and leave, Shay grabbed his arm and plastered herself against him. If the woman got any closer she'd be on top of him. "Sing a duet with me, Jamie."

When he started to protest Shay struck a pose and pouted. "Please? Come on, cowboy. You were so awesome. I'd love to sing with you. We could make beautiful music together."

Brother. Did the woman think that ridiculous pretty-girl routine actually worked with men? Emma grimaced. Of course Shay did, because usually all the stacked blonde had to do was stick out her double Ds and wet her lips, and men trampled each other to do her bidding.

"Poor Jamie. The night just keeps getting worse. Now Shay's got her sights on him," Avery said.

"Poor us, is more like it. Obviously you don't remember how she sings. A cat screeching because its tail got caught under a rocking chair sounds better than she does." Emma shook her head. "If she gets any closer to him, we'll all get an entirely different kind of show."

The crowd joined in shouting for Jamie to sing again. He tried to wiggle free of Shay's grasp, but instead of letting go she held on like a puppy with a brand-new toy.

"Mick, cue up 'Let's Make Love' by Faith Hill and Tim McGraw." Shay leaned back on her heels, her ample chest practically shoved in Jamie's face as she looked the man up one side and down the other.

Emma nearly choked on her sip of beer. Could the woman be any more obvious? She might as well ask him to get a room.

When Shay and Jamie started singing, Avery leaned closer to Emma. "I thought you were kidding about how bad her voice was. The dogs howling in the shelter are more in tune than she is. Not that the men around here seem to notice."

"Her voice isn't the asset they're concentrating on." Emma winced as Shay hit another clinker. "With the way she's bouncing around up there, it's a wonder she hasn't popped right out of that low-cut sweater."

"She does like to put everything on display, doesn't she? Her bra must be industrial strength."

Unlike most of the men in Halligan's, Jamie looked less than pleased with Shay's display. He kept trying to slide away from her, only to have her follow him.

"Emma, I can't take any more of that caterwauling," Mick said when he appeared beside her. "You've got to go onstage to rescue Jamie before we either go deaf from listening to that harebrained female or she gets us raided."

"Don't tell me *your* grandson can't handle a woman?" she said.

"Come on, Em," Avery added. "I think it would be cool to hear you two sing together. Consider it your good deed for the day."

"That was fun. Let's do another," Shay said the moment the song ended, her voice all bright and airy.

"We need to give someone else a chance. Who else wants to sing?" Jamie pleaded, a look of desperation crossing his features when he glanced in Emma's direction.

How could she ignore that lost-puppy look after what he'd done for her this afternoon?

"Jamie, sing something else," Cathy Hughes, one of Halligan's waitresses, said as she served another round of drinks to a stage-side table.

"I'll sing as long as you sing with me, Jamie," Doreen Stone called out, a dreamy look her husband, Joshua, wouldn't appreciate plastered on her face.

"Help me out, Emma," Mick pleaded, as a heated discussion flared up between Shay and Doreen about who should perform with Jamie. "I'm afraid they're going to go at each other or start tearing at Jamie. I've never seen the women here act like this before. It's downright scary."

"Okay. I'll do it." She turned to Mick. "But you have to get Shay off the stage. I'm not fighting that battle."

"I think you could take her," Avery teased.

"My money would be on you, too, but I'll handle Shay," Mick said. "I don't want any trouble."

Once she and Mick made their way to the stage, Emma picked up a mic and waited nearby while he pried Shay's hand off Jamie's arm. "It's my place, and I want to hear Emma and Jamie sing 'Jackson.' I think they'll do June and Johnny proud." Then he practically dragged Shay off the stage.

When Emma joined Jamie, he smiled. A simple thing. No big deal, and yet her heart fluttered. With his voice, looks and that smile, he would drive women crazy.

Don't let him get to you. You've sworn off musicians, remember?

Jamie put the mic behind his back and leaned toward her. His warm breath fanned against her skin, sending little ripples of delight through her. "Thanks for being part of the rescue posse. The way she was pawing me, I was worried she was going to slip a five in my pants any minute."

His comment made her think of the movie *Magic Mike*. Bad idea. The image of Jamie dressed in Matthew McConaughey's getup of tight jeans, leather vest and cowboy hat in that movie flashed in her mind. Emma swallowed hard and sweat trickled between her breasts.

Jamie Westland would make one fine-looking cowboy.

"You ready?" he asked.

She stared at him and tried to swallow the lump in her throat. She was ready for any number of things, none of which were appropriate for the stage. "Excuse me?"

"Are you ready for Mick to cue up the music?"

All she could do was nod. When the familiar tune filled the room she relaxed. Now in her element, she glanced at the crowd and slipped into performance mode. When she and Jamie started singing, her body moved to the music. Their voices melded. His presence beside her felt comfortable, and yet not. By the time they reached the first chorus, she knew she'd made a big mistake agreeing to sing with Jamie.

Big? More like monumental. Or catastrophic.

Because all Emma could think about was how she hadn't felt this connected to anyone in a long time, and that was not a good thing.

Chapter Five

Mick stared at his grandson on the stage with Emma and felt as if he was looking at a younger version of himself. He may not have been a part of Jamie's life for eighteen years, but no doubt about it, the bloodline ran true.

Listening to Jamie sing, Mick knew his grandson could still have a performing career in music. If he wanted to. Jamie could have the choices he'd never had. The sparks between his grandson and Emma lit up the place. If things got any hotter he'd have to turn up the air-conditioning.

If he hadn't known these two belonged together before, he sure as hell would now. There was a chemistry between Jamie and Emma that couldn't be manufactured and everyone in the room knew it. They had that rare something that some couples just had. Johnny Cash and June Carter Cash. George Jones and Tammy Wynette. Faith Hill and Tim McGraw.

Out of the corner of his eye, Mick spotted Cody, one of his busboys, and called him over. Whenever the teenager got a break, he was always showing Mick funny videos he found on the internet. "You can take videos on that phone of yours, can't you?"

"I'd never take any videos here at work. Did someone say I did?" the gangly redhead said, fear making his voice crack.

"Don't worry. You're not in trouble," Mick rushed to reassure the teen who'd nearly started shaking in his boots. "I want you to video Emma and Jamie on-stage and post it on that video site you're always talking about."

"YouTube?"

"That's the one. You keep that thing running the whole time they're onstage or until your battery runs out."

"You sure? It's crazy busy in here. Cathy will have my head if I don't clear her tables."

"I'll take care of busing the tables."

"Okay, you're the boss." Cody handed Mick his tub of dishes and headed toward the stage, cell phone in hand.

Mick smiled. If he was right about Emma and Jamie, once people saw the video they'd start clamoring to see the pair onstage again. Emma wouldn't be able to resist that. Once he got them working together, then they'd realize they could be good together off the stage, as well. His plan was coming right along.

JAMIE WASN'T SURE he'd ever felt this alive. While things had started out rocky with him stumbling over the words, now that he'd gotten into the song he felt at home onstage. Of course having Emma beside him helped.

Confident, dynamic and sexy as hell, she made a man come alive just by being in the same room. She was like a lightning bug on a dark summer night—all bright energy, flitting all over the place, shining on everyone and everything and just as hard to contain.

Emma's voice flowed through and around him. Her

green eyes sparkled with excitement and drew him in. He glanced at the screen to check the lyrics, then he leaned toward her, smiling as he sang about how he'd teach the women in Jackson a thing or two. Then she took over the song taunting about how she'd be dancing on a pony keg and he'd be a hound with his tail tucked between his legs.

Her eyes flashed with amusement, and he could see her doing just what she said—dancing and sending him on a merry chase. He laughed and wondered when he'd had this much fun. The fact that he couldn't remember left him oddly disturbed.

A minute later when the song ended the thunderous applause and exuberant hoots broke the connection between them. He'd been completely lost in Emma and the song. He stood there staring at the crowd, shocked both at their reaction and his. Definitely not the restrained approval he was accustomed to receiving from symphony patrons.

His chest rose and fell with his heavy breathing. His body hummed in a way it hadn't in years.

Someone in the crowd shouted for him and Emma to sing another song. He turned to the woman beside him. Her smile taunted him. "What do you say? Should we give 'em what they want?"

"Why not?" Her skin glistening from exertion, her eyes twinkled like emeralds when she grinned. Then she slowly looked him up and down from head to toe, and damned if he didn't feel himself blush. "The question is, city boy, can you keep up with this cowgirl?"

"I can take anything you dish out."

The crowd oohed at his challenge. Jamie froze. He'd forgotten about the mic in his hand and that everyone could hear their exchange. This woman could make him forgot his own name.

"Then let's see what you've got, city boy. Mick, cue up another song."

More cheers came from the audience.

He and Emma sang five more songs before Mick joined them. "As great as it's been having Jamie and Emma up here, the band's arrived." When some of the crowd started to grumble, Mick added, "I think these two need to come back real soon and sing again. What do you think?"

More cheers and whistles came from the crowd as he and Emma left the stage, and Jamie realized he wasn't ready to let her go. He wanted to hang on to this energy, to how she made him feel, as though he could storm the castle and come away the victor. "Let me buy you a drink."

"I could use a big glass of ice water."

"Wow, you're a cheap date."

The joy he'd seen in her eyes on the stage died, and the bond between them evaporated, leaving her looking at him as if he was the gum stuck to the bottom of her boots. Maybe it was the date comment. That dented his ego. He rushed to salvage his pride. "There's no reason for you to get all out of joint. I'm not hitting on you. My mom raised me better than that. Let me get you that water. I don't know about you, but I just sweated off five pounds on the stage."

Great way to impress a girl. Tell her you're hot, sweaty and smelly. You're still on that great roll from this afternoon, buddy.

"People don't realize how much water weight performers lose onstage. Lead the way."

They started to make their way to the bar, but only

went a few feet before someone stopped them to say how much they enjoyed their singing. Another couple of steps and they repeated the process. When the third group of people waylaid them, Jamie turned to Emma and said, "I say head down and we make a run for the bar. Stop for nothing, or we're going to die of thirst." He grabbed her hand. "Coming through." Someone tried to catch his attention. "Sorry. Join us at the bar if you want to talk. The lady's about to collapse from dehydration." He kept moving forward until they reached the bar.

"That was subtle, and not the least bit overly dramatic." Emma shook her head and sank onto an empty bar stool.

"I got the job done, so quit complaining," Jamie said as he moved behind the bar beside Mick. Once there he plucked a glass off the shelf, filled it with ice and water and placed it in front of Emma. "And now I'm back to bartender."

"Thanks for filling in, you two." Mick patted Jamie on the back.

"The credit goes to Emma. She was the one who knew what to do. I followed her lead."

"You were amazing, Jamie. I haven't heard anybody sound that good in years," one of the women seated at the bar said. Jamie wasn't sure which one, not that he cared. All he noticed was how quiet Emma had become.

"That was because of Emma. Anyone singing with her would sound like a star." Jamie reached for another glass.

"You two were almost as good as June and Johnny," the man sitting next to Emma said.

She smiled at him, but her eyes failed to light up as they had earlier. She sat with her back ramrod-straight, her hand clutching her water glass. Something wasn't right. "That's very sweet of you to say so, Henry. I'm glad you enjoyed it."

"We need to have these two back, boss," Cathy said after she ordered two beers and a whiskey neat for one of her tables. "I bet we'd pack the place, and I could rake in some heavy-duty tips."

"Are you trying to tell us something?" Henry teased.

"You're a good tipper, but let's face it. People open their wallets wider when they're all toe-tapping happy from good music." She patted Emma's arm. "Hearing you and Jamie sing sure makes my night go faster. Say you two will come back again."

"Maroon Peak Pass and the shelter keep me pretty busy, but I'll see what we can do."

Jamie couldn't miss the lack of enthusiasm in Emma's voice. In other words, don't call us, we'll call you. Here he thought they'd shared something special on-stage, but apparently he was the only one who thought so.

"Have you had any luck finding a fiddle player to replace Molly? I bet that's weighing on you since the contest at the state fair is coming up quick," Henry said.

Emma shook her head. "I've contacted anyone who might know of someone, and I've spent hours searching the internet. It's downright scary what some people think passes for music."

"What's this about a contest?" Jamie asked.

"The state fair is having a competition." Emma explained how the winner got a private consultation with Phillip Brandise, one of the biggest producers in country music. "If we impress him, we have a good shot at him offering us a recording contract."

"Will not having a violinist hurt your chances?" Jamie asked as he poured the beers for Cathy.

"Not if I can help it." He wanted to smile at Emma's grit, clearly evident in the stubborn tilt of her chin and the determination in her voice. The woman might bend, but she wouldn't break.

"Maybe you don't have to go without one. How about Jamie?" Henry nodded in his direction. "You play the fiddle, don't you?"

"Since I was eight. I was one of those geeky kids who spent the afternoon inside practicing the violin."

"You should get Jamie to take Molly's place." Henry took a long draw on his beer and leaned back in his seat, obviously pleased with himself. "Then you two could sing together all the time."

He mulled the idea over. Being onstage with Emma had been the most fun he'd had in a long time. He could help her out while getting the challenge of learning something new. Granted, learning country music wouldn't be a huge one—how hard could it be for someone who'd been classically trained?—but it would be something *different,* and that's what he needed right now. He'd fill up some of his empty time and get the added bonus of exercising and strengthening his hand. As far as he could see it was a win all around.

"You could at least help out until Emma finds someone." Henry turned to Emma, a big uneven smile on his face. "Isn't that a great idea?"

Jamie glanced at her, about to say they should give Henry's idea a try, but the words stuck in his throat. She'd pressed her lips together so hard they were a thin white line. She clutched her water glass so tight the tendons in her hand stood out.

"It's something to consider, but I'll have to think about it since Jamie doesn't have any experience—"

"I've got a degree from Juilliard and played with the

New York Philharmonic." His words came out harsher than he intended. Her comment shouldn't have nicked his pride, but it had. "I'd call that experience."

"If you'd let me finish, what I was going to say was you don't have any experience playing with a country band."

She really thought what she'd added would make the insult sting less? "I think I can handle it."

"Just because you possess the skills to play the notes doesn't mean you can make *music*. Everyone thinks country music is easy to play, but it's not. It's filled with heart. It's storytelling set to music. That's what makes it special. If someone doesn't feel the connection, it doesn't work. What you create is just noise."

Wood creaked as people shifted awkwardly on the bar stools.

"I happen to like country music. It has an honesty that resonates with people. Me included."

"Again, that doesn't mean you can play it on a professional level. The business is very competitive."

He shrugged, but all he could think about was grabbing her and kissing her long and hard until neither one of them had the energy to carry on this conversation. "Good luck at the state fair."

"Okay, you two," Mick said as he rushed over from the far side of the bar. "I think it's time to change the subject. Jamie, let's get everyone here at the bar another round on me."

Cheers and whoops circled around the bar. The only one besides him who didn't seem happy was Emma as she stalked away to rejoin her friends.

Sunday afternoon Emma sank onto her couch in her living room, a cup of herbal tea beside her as she tried to focus on the sheet music spread out on the coffee table in front of her. Unfortunately all she could think about was how she'd gone off the deep end last night with Jamie.

She'd been so far off her game yesterday she hadn't even been able to see the stadium. That feeling started when she arrived at Halligan's for the auditions and found Jamie there, and the day had continued to spiral out of control. She'd been strung pretty tight by the time she'd sung with him, and hadn't been prepared for her reaction. The excitement, the electricity, the elation. She hadn't had that kind of chemistry onstage in years. Since Tucker. That left her shaking in her favorite boots.

Follow that with how crazy everyone had gone over their performance and half the town jumping on the she-should-let-Jamie-play-with-*her*-band bandwagon, and the perfect storm had formed inside her. And boy, had she let loose on Jamie. The poor guy hadn't deserved that.

As if she didn't have enough distractions to keep her from getting anything productive done, her cell phone rang. Glancing at the screen revealed Avery's name.

"I wanted to make sure you were okay. What happened at the bar between you and Jamie? You scurried out of there so fast I didn't get to ask," Avery said when Emma answered.

"Scurried? I don't scurry."

"Stomped? Charged? Either of those work? And don't avoid the question."

Emma rubbed the knot in her shoulder, trying to ease the tension there. "I have no idea what happened. I was doing okay."

Okay? You were having more fun, were more alive and happier than you've been in years.

"When Jamie and I were done singing everyone kept saying how great we sounded. Like I sounded lousy before or something. Then Henry Alvarez had the bright idea for Jamie to replace Molly in the band. I said something that Jamie took the wrong way." But what had she expected him to do? Only someone deaf, dumb and blind would've taken a statement that started out with the words *you have no experience* as anything but an insult. "Then it was like we were both possessed, or we lost all common sense and self-control. I don't know. It was crazy. All of a sudden he and I were arguing like two children over who got the bigger piece of cake."

"Having Jamie replace Molly isn't a bad idea."

"Don't start. I can't take it today. I need the I-support-you-in-whatever-decision-you-make speech."

"Then you aren't going to be happy about what's happening on Facebook this morning. You and Jamie have created quite a stir. Someone posted a video of you two singing."

No. Everyone in Halligan's nagging her was one thing, but opening the mess up to the entire free world via the internet? Please, no. Emma booted up her computer and logged on to the social media site. The first thing she noticed was Shay had posted a video of her own performance with Jamie along with a comment about how they had sounded "magical." Really? "I can't believe Shay has the nerve to call her caterwauling with Jamie 'magical.' The woman is either delusional or tone-deaf. Not that anyone's called her on that."

Instead all the comments were from women who went all dreamy over Jamie, his "see into a woman's soul" eyes, his "make me swoon" voice and his "I want to cuddle up with that" body.

"Forget about Shay's post. Have you found the one of your performance with Jamie?"

She located the video. Her stomach dropped when she saw how many likes and shares they had. "I can't believe it. We promoted the heck out of the band's last video, and this thing's gotten more plays in one day than we got in a month."

"If this keeps up you could get some great exposure."

Emma hit Play. As the video started all the excitement she'd felt with Jamie rushed back. She knew it felt right being onstage with him, but she'd had no idea how the energy crackled between them, elevating their performance and their vocals, infusing their singing with a sizzling sensuality. She'd been wrong. She'd never had this kind of chemistry with anyone.

She read the comments. People compared them to some of country's great duos. Her mind rebelled at the thought. She refused to tie her career to one person, especially a man. That's why she'd started Maroon Peak Pass, and why she was the lead singer. Bass players, drummers and fiddle players could be replaced. Not quickly, as she was learning from Molly's departure. But relying on someone else left her vulnerable, something she refused to do again.

"Promise you won't bite my head off if I ask you a certain question you're not going to like me asking, but I have to ask because it's in the shelter's best interest."

"Avery, it's Sunday afternoon, and my brain's in weekend mode. I have no idea what you just said."

"Don't get mad, but I think we should ask Jamie to sing at the shelter fund-raiser."

"Why would I get upset about that? From the interest he's generated online, I think that's a great idea. He could draw more people to the event." Young, single, man-hungry women, but, hey, their money bought dog food and cat litter as well as anyone else's.

"The thing is, he needs a band to play for him. I was thinking he could sing with Maroon Peak Pass."

Chapter Six

"Just think about it for a minute before you say no," Avery said.

"I don't need to. You want him to sing. That's fine with me, but have him do karaoke again."

"While everyone enjoyed Jamie's singing, they loved you two singing *together* more. Remember the first time Reed and I danced at Halligan's? You told me things were so hot between us you almost ran for a fire extinguisher."

Emma didn't like where the conversation was headed. "Uh-huh."

"I thought the same thing when you and Jamie were onstage."

"That was before our disagreement. I think what we said to each other effectively killed any attraction." *Liar.* At least it hadn't dampened her fascination. "Avery, it was awful. It's not like me to be that thoughtless and hurt someone."

And she had. She'd seen the shock wash over Jamie's features after her "no experience" comment. Then, as she'd continued to lob grenades in his direction, the expression on his face had let her know she'd hit her target. "I wish I could take it all back. We just seemed to push each other's hot buttons."

"That's because there's major sparks between you two."

That's what she was afraid of. She'd always had trouble separating the chemistry she felt with a man onstage from real life. She couldn't afford to make another mistake, not after she'd finally gotten her feet under her and her career back on track.

"You said something else to me that night that fits here."

"I have the funny feeling you're going to throw something I said back in my face."

"You've got that right."

"Your situation with Reed was different. He was an old boyfriend. One you never got over."

"That may be, but I'm going to tell you what you said to me anyway because somewhere along the line you forgot about having a life."

"You're right. After Mom died I should've packed up my Camry and headed back to Nashville." At first she'd been too drained to start over, knowing she'd have to find a new day job, an apartment and, toughest of all, a new band. Instead she'd insisted the smart plan was to take time to grieve and regroup. The next thing she knew another year had gone by. "I may not have the life I envisioned, but I have a life."

"That sounds familiar," Avery said. "Should I tell you what you said to me?"

You forgot about having a love life.

She hated when her words came back to bite her on the ass, and these left teeth marks.

While what Avery said about her love life was true, Emma had consciously made the choice. Women couldn't have it all. That was just a bill of goods the media and big business sold them to keep females from grumbling too much.

For women who wanted to be movers and shakers at the top of their profession, something had to give. Either work or family had to come first. That is, if a woman was lucky enough to find a man who could handle her success, and there weren't many of those around. If she wanted a guy who'd be faithful and didn't have horns and a tail, she narrowed the field even further. But say she won the lottery and found such a man. If she wanted to compete with the big boys in her field, her home life would have to take a backseat. That eventually caused problems. A man might understand for a while, but eventually he'd complain, forcing her to choose between him and her career.

"We've known each other most of our lives, and I've seen you change over the past few years," Avery continued, her voice hesitant but devoid of judgment. "You've shut yourself off from everyone."

"That's not true. I have some close friends. One of whom doesn't know what she's talking about right now."

"It's not just with friends."

"I don't need a man in my life. I've got enough problems."

"You don't let anyone get close to you anymore. I didn't realize it until I saw you onstage at Halligan's, but you've shut down so much emotionally it's changing your music. When you were singing with Jamie, you let your guard down. You were real. I think that's what made that night so special for everyone watching you two."

Emma's hand tightened around her phone. Avery's words rippled through her like a virus, invading and pervasive, altering everything they touched. Had she changed that much since she'd come back from Nash-ville this time?

Since returning she hadn't connected with many of her old friends. She hadn't wanted to. In the past she and her bandmates had become friends, but not this time. She rarely socialized, except when Avery cajoled her into going out as only a best friend could. She hadn't gone on a single date, either.

The thought sank in. She hadn't gone out on a date in over two years? That explained a lot of her current prob-lem with Jamie. No wonder seeing him—a guy who, if anything, was hotter than he'd been at nineteen—and remembering how young and hopeful she'd been with him left her reeling. Then add in her memories of how he kissed better than any man had a right to legally, and no wonder her hormones had come out of hibernation.

Avery's words continued to hammer at Emma, breaking through to the truth. She'd been so weary, so beat down from her mother's illness and death, Clint's rejection and having to start over careerwise that she'd gone into survival mode emotionally. She'd quit feel-ing anything.

Until Jamie.

"Fate sometimes brings people into our lives for a reason," Avery said.

"Don't give me that philosophical bull. My life doesn't need changing. It's fine the way it is."

You're protesting too much. Who are you trying so hard to convince?

"Do you think that's why Jamie pushes your hot but-tons so easily? Are you so sure your life doesn't need shaking up?"

La, la, la. I'm not listening. I won't. I can't.

Wasn't it bad enough that Jamie had invaded her

weekend, her Facebook news feed and way too many of her thoughts? Now Avery wanted her to let him into her one haven, Maroon Peak Pass.

"With my mom's death and all that's happened over the past two years, I'm not sure I'm strong enough to take my life being shaken up. I couldn't even take it being stirred right now." She chuckled at her lame joke, but the sound came out nervous, almost fragile.

"Then forget about Jamie singing at the fund-raiser. Sure, money's tight at the shelter. When isn't it?" Avery said, executing an abrupt about-face. "But it's not like when we needed to buy the land last year. We'll be fine. You backed me up when I bent the rules about Jess volunteering without an adult because I couldn't face Reed. Now I'm returning the favor."

Tears stung Emma's eyes. She bit the inside of her cheek, trying to regain control as she stumbled into the bathroom for a tissue. "If I were the perfect employee I'd say I'll suck it up, take one for the team and let Jamie play with us because it's best for the shelter."

"So you'll have to settle for being nearly perfect."

"Thanks." She caught sight of herself in the vanity mirror. Who was that woman staring back at her? The one with the wide, haunted eyes who looked as if she was scared of her own shadow. No one she recognized, that's for sure.

That'd be the day, and no way would she let the shelter lose out on money because she was scared of being attracted to a man.

Sometimes fighting against something was worse than giving in. She'd learned that one year when she'd given up carbs for Lent. The cravings had just about driven her crazy. That's when she learned moderation was the key to almost everything in life. This situation with Jamie wouldn't get the best of her. The key was control and moderate doses. "I've changed my mind about having Jamie sing. If you want him to do a couple of numbers, the band will back him up, but I want it duly noted that my status has changed from nearly perfect to perfect employee."

"Done. I owe you one."

"That's for sure."

After her conversation with Avery, Emma worked on returning emails from prospective volunteers, but messages started popping up on her personal Facebook page. Was Jamie single? Could she introduce them?

She closed her personal page and continued working on shelter business. That worked for five minutes until her phone started dinging with text messages from friends and acquaintances asking the same questions. Lord, you'd think Jamie was the last single man in a four-state area from the feeding frenzy he'd created.

Deciding to put a stop to the nonsense, she pulled up her Facebook page and posted a statement on her wall. I have two jobs. Running a dating service isn't one of them. If that changes, I'll let everyone know.

She chewed on her lip for a minute thinking about the video of her and Jamie on YouTube, and she started wondering what he was like onstage with the Philharmonic. Out of curiosity she entered his name on Google. When the results popped up she clicked on a link of him playing a solo. A minute later all she could think was that she was an idiot to have scoffed at Henry's suggestion.

Jamie's musical ability made Molly look like a middle schooler who'd picked up the violin a month ago. And she'd had the nerve to tell him just because he had the skill to play the notes didn't mean he could make music. With his talent, merely playing the notes would outshine anyone she'd auditioned. Anyone she could hope to find.

She'd never seriously considered asking Jamie because she'd been too busy running from what she felt for him, but now that she stepped back and analyzed the situation, the idea of him joining the band had merit. She'd been searching for something or someone to grab people's attention and set her band apart. Molly's fiddle playing helped, but not as much as she'd hoped. Between Jamie's charisma and his talent, could he be the answer?

While Emma had struggled to create a presence on social media, Jamie had accomplished more for Maroon Peak Pass in one day than she had with all her efforts, and the more buzz they had going into the state fair, the better their chances that Phillip Brandise would have them on his radar before they played a note.

But working with Jamie? If only he hadn't made her go all weak in the knees and warm and tingly everywhere else. Talk about a job-related hazard.

She opened a new document on her computer and listed the pros and cons of working with Jamie. The first thing she wrote under the con column was that to get him to even listen to her offer after the way she'd acted would mean letting go of her pride. *Major groveling involved.* She stared at what she'd typed and underlined *major.* Halfway through her list she realized the best thing for the band was to ask Jamie to join them, but maybe Luke and Grayson would feel differently. After all, she hadn't been thinking all that clearly since she'd picked Jamie up at the airport.

Hoping she was wrong about him and the band, she fired off an email with the link to his solo and the pros and cons of her idea—sans the her having to grovel part—to Luke and Grayson for their opinion. Maybe they'd respond saying she'd lost her mind and no way could a classical musician make the transition to country music. Then she could let go of the idea and if anyone brought the subject up again, she could say she and the band had discussed the issue. Case closed.

Five minutes later both Luke and Grayson had responded saying they thought asking Jamie was a great idea.

Now what?

SUNDAY NIGHT WHEN the restlessness hit, Jamie set out for a walk. When the hike through the mountains failed to burn off his agitation, he headed for the barn to muck out a few stalls.

How had he let Emma get under his skin so many ways last night? Lack of self-control. Loneliness. Insanity. Take your pick.

He scooped up a forkful of hay and dumped it into the bin on the far wall of the stall. Bits of straw floated around him, eventually landing on his running shoes. The shoes worked great for jogging through the city, but weren't so hot for ranch work. He should think about investing in a good pair of boots, but he'd held off. He kept telling himself he wouldn't be around that long. Or at least he hoped not. There was something about investing in work boots that made him feel as though he was admitting his situation wouldn't change, that his hand wouldn't improve. Right now he preferred to think of being in Colorado as a vacation, as a distraction from the problems in his life.

And that's what Emma was. One powerful distraction. He retrieved more hay and scattered it around the stall. He wished he could see in a crystal ball and know if all his hand needed was hard work and time. Until he figured that out, he was in limbo. As if he'd been cut adrift and was floating through life wherever the current took him.

When his cell phone rang, he glanced at his watch, smiled and leaned the pitch fork against the barn wall. Eight on Sunday night. His parents were right on time with their weekly call.

"How are things going in Colorado?" his dad asked.

"Getting away has cleared my head." *Too bad it's now as empty as a ski resort in summer.*

For the next few minutes they discussed his dad's job and how work was going for his mom at the accounting firm. He got the latest news about his sisters, discovering Kate was up for a promotion with 3M.

"I think Wade is going to propose to Rachel soon," his mom said. "Maybe we'll be having a wedding in the spring."

Yup, his sisters had all their ducks in a row. Their lives neatly falling into place. Yet another way he and his siblings differed.

"So, you've been working around the ranch and at the restaurant?" his mother asked, obviously trolling for information.

He told them about getting roped into singing karaoke when the band was late. "It turned out to be a lot of fun. Emma, that girl I dated a couple of times that one summer, sang with me. We were pretty good together."

In more ways than just onstage.

"I'm glad you're getting out and socializing. It's funny that you mentioned karaoke. You used to love singing," his mother said. "Remember how much you enjoyed singing in the church choir?"

"For a while there we weren't sure whether you'd focus on the violin or singing," his dad added.

He'd forgotten about the children's choir he'd been in when he was in elementary school. He'd wanted to take choir in middle school, but couldn't fit it, orchestra and his core classes into his schedule. He'd been forced to choose, but there'd been no real choice. All his teachers agreed that while his singing was good, he was a gifted violinist.

He hadn't considered singing anywhere but the shower since then. Until last night. First Mick mentioned him playing country music. Then Henry suggested he join Emma's band and now his parents mentioned how much he once loved singing. Maybe fate was trying to tell him something.

"I never understood why schools make kids choose between choir and instruments in middle school," his father said. "Those kids who want to have a career in music should be able to do both."

"I say you should quit worrying about the future so much right now. Have some fun. Life has a way of working out if we give it time." His mother's soothing voice flowed over him. For a pencil-pushing number cruncher, she had a knack for knowing just what to say.

"You'll figure things out. We have faith in you," his father said. "We'll support you no matter what you decide to do. All we want is for you to be happy."

He'd hit the lottery when they'd chosen him, he thought as he ended the call and shoved his cell phone into his back pocket. He was about to head back to the house when he heard Trixie rustling around in her stall. Sensing that something was off, he decided to check on her. When he opened the stall door, the horse swung her head and turned her rear toward him, blocking the entrance. "What's bothering you, girl?"

A couple of Mick's horses leaned toward being high-strung, but not Trixie. The chestnut loved everyone. Of all the horses on the ranch, Trixie was his favorite. Something about her gentle spirit mixed with her curious nature and her calm strength tugged at him. But right now she was definitely out of sorts. Ears back, she moved her head up and down as if nodding. One of the first things Mick had taught him was how to recognize when a horse sent out don't-come-any-closer signals, and Trixie was saying that loud and clear.

Time to tread easy. The most laid-back animals often created the biggest storms when they got upset.

Kind of like a certain woman he'd irritated at Halligan's.

He still couldn't figure out what had happened with Emma. They'd been great together onstage, teasing and joking. Playing off each other, sometimes in such a sensual dance he'd forgotten they were in public. But the minute the music had ended, things changed. Emma had almost shut down before his eyes. At least until Henry had suggested he join her band. That comment sure lit a fire under her, and if the truth be told, some of what she'd said stirred him up pretty good, too.

They'd both let their tempers get the best of them.

He was just about to head out of the stall when a weak, squeaky noise came from the far corner. "What's over there, girl, and why won't you let me see?" He managed to peer around the horse at the hay pile. There he spotted a small bundle of white-and-tan fur. When the animal wiggled he realized it was a puppy. A very young one that needed its mother.

"So that's what you're protecting." Not sure what else

to do, he pulled out his cell phone and called Mick. "I found a pup in Trixie's stall. One too young to be on its own. Do you know who it might belong to or where we could find its mother?"

"I don't know of anyone around here that had a pregnant dog or one that had puppies recently. The mom's probably a stray and the one you found got separated from her and the rest of the litter."

"We can't just leave it here. From the way it's crying it's either hungry or hurt."

"Bring the pup to the house. I'll call Emma. She works at the animal shelter. She'll know what to do."

"Trixie won't let me anywhere near it."

"Then Emma will have to come out here and help us get the poor thing."

Chapter Seven

Standing in his living room, Mick smiled so big he thought he might bust. He couldn't have planned this better.

Most of the day he'd been racking his brain to figure out how to fix things between Emma and Jamie. Now the perfect solution had dropped into his lap, or rather crawled into his barn.

"We don't need to bother Emma," Jamie said. "You and I can get the pup out and drop it off at the shelter."

Sure, they could, but that wouldn't get his match-making plans back on track.

"I don't feel comfortable handling this. Better safe than sorry, I say. Emma deals with stuff like this at the shelter all the time," Mick said with confidence even though he had no idea how many rescue situations Emma dealt with since she was the volunteer coordinator. Hopefully Jamie wouldn't think of that.

"Okay, you're the boss."

Mick smiled again as he ended the conversation with Jamie and called Emma. This would work. When she came to help with the pup he'd make himself scarce, forcing her and Jamie to work together. Taking care of the dog would give them a chance to get to know each other. It would give them something other than music to talk about.

"Jamie and I need some help with a pup we found in the barn," he said when she answered.

"The shelter's closed, but I'll meet you there to accept the puppy."

"The problem is the dog's in Trixie's stall, and she won't let us near it."

"I'll relay the information to Avery and have her call you. She'll know what to do. Since she's the vet, she handles these calls. That way if the animal needs immediate medical attention she can take care of it."

Damn. He should've thought about that problem before he called. He scrambled to think of a reason to get Emma to come out with Avery, but couldn't come up with anything on the fly. "Will you call me back after you talk to her?"

That would at least buy him some time.

EMMA SAT ON her couch and realized she'd actually be glad when her weekend ended and she could return to work. Maybe then she could forget about Jamie Westland.

At least the issue with the puppy would be Avery's problem. Or so she thought, but by the third ring when Avery hadn't picked up, Emma started getting nervous. After the fourth ring, Avery's voice mail kicked in, forcing her to leave a message about the situation. Then she waited.

Where was Avery and why wasn't her phone on? That wasn't like her. After ten minutes when she hadn't heard, Emma started thinking she needed to go out to the ranch. If the puppy was as young as Mick said, it could quickly become dehydrated without nursing. Then if it was flea infested, which was highly likely if it was a stray, it could be anemic and worm-riddled. Combine all those conditions and the situation could turn dire for a young puppy surprisingly fast.

After ten on Sunday night and now she was dealing with an orphaned puppy. That she could handle, but this wasn't a simple drop-off. Unwilling to put the puppy at risk, she snatched her cell phone off the coffee table and called Mick. "I had to leave a message for Avery. Are you sure you can't get to the puppy?"

Please say you've gotten it out of the stall.

"I really think we need another person. That way Jamie and I can deal with Trixie while you get the pup. Otherwise I'm worried the little fella will get hurt. Jamie said it looks like it's just starting to walk and who knows how long it's been since the pup's eaten."

"I'm on my way."

As she drove across town toward Mick's ranch, she told herself she'd stay a few minutes. Tops. That's all this little task should take. After all, Mick had a solid plan. He and Jamie would calm the horse while she scooted around to scoop up the puppy. No problem. Then she'd get back in her car and head for the shelter before they finished thanking her.

Confident that she could handle the situation, Emma's thoughts turned to dealing with seeing Jamie again. She prided herself on being pretty easygoing. She understood people, cut them slack and didn't let them get to her. That was part of what made her a good volunteer coordinator. But she couldn't figure Jamie out. He was such an odd combination. Distant and formal one minute, and then—she paused—hot, steamy and sexy as hell the next.

Well, there wouldn't be any of that tonight. As far

as she was concerned he was just another person who needed help with a stray animal. She dealt with this on a daily basis, but to make sure nothing went wrong, she'd avoid the hot-button topics—politics, religion and, in her case, music. And if he threw her any of those turn-a-woman-to-warm-goo looks like he had on the stage, she'd just close her eyes.

By the time she reached Mick's ranch, she had a smile plastered on her face and an I-can-handle-this mantra running through her head. She took two calming breaths and tugged open the barn door. The hinges squeaked, announcing her arrival.

The familiar smells of her childhood—hay, dust and horses—swirled around her as she followed the low rumble of male voices until she located Jamie and Mick. She rounded the corner and froze. All her confidence rushed out of her, along with her breath, when she spotted Jamie. Nothing made a handsome man look quite the way a good pair of jeans did, and Jamie was no exception.

Remember, he's just another person with an orphaned animal. Granted, a better-looking one than most, but he's just another person who needs help.

He nodded in her direction. "Thanks for coming."

"We sure do appreciate it," Mick said when she reached them. Then he patted Jamie on the back. "I'm sure you two can handle this, so I'll head back to the house."

"Wait a minute. Stop right there," Emma said when Mick turned to leave. "You said we needed all three of us to handle this."

"That's right. I did." The older man pushed bits of hay around with the toe of his scuffed boot. Then a second later he snapped his fingers. "We're gonna need a halter. I'll go get one."

"We'll be fine without it."

"Things will be easier if we use one," Mick said as he dashed off.

She turned to Jamie. "Is it just me, or is he acting a little odd?"

"You think?" Jamie shook his head. "I'm sorry Mick bothered you. I told him we could handle this, but he was worried about something happening to the dog." Jamie shoved his hands into the front pockets of his jeans. The movement pulled his dark T-shirt taunt across his broad shoulders.

For a city boy he sure looked comfortable in the barn. Comfortable? No, that wasn't right. He looked as if he belonged on a cowboy-of-the-month calendar. All he needed was a cowboy hat dangling from his long fingers and a good pair of boots. She hadn't expected that. How could a man be at ease on a symphony stage and equally so in a barn?

She tried to focus her thoughts. This would be a lot easier if she cleared the air. "About last night. I need to apologize. My mouth was driving while my brain was asleep at the wheel. Could we just forget the whole thing?"

Relief eased the tension in his face. "That's fine with me. I said some things I'm not real proud of."

Puppy whimpers followed by Trixie's nervous movements drifted out of the stall. "Where's Mick with the halter?" Jamie glanced down the hallway.

The sooner they retrieved the puppy, the sooner she could hightail it out of here. "We can manage without him. Do you want to deal with the horse or get the dog?"

"I'll handle Trixie. She and I are friends, aren't we, girl?"

Emma swallowed hard. *I bet you are. What female wouldn't respond to a good-looking man when he gazed at her with those dreamy brown eyes and whispered her name in that bedroom voice?*

"When you get in the stall, talk to the horse in a calm, soothing voice until you can get close enough to stroke her neck and face. That should keep her relaxed enough for me to get the puppy."

As Jamie turned and walked toward the stall, Emma had to remind herself to breathe. What his butt did for those jeans ought to be registered as an illegal weapon. *Breathe in and out.* Maybe concentrating on that would get her surging hormones under control.

When he tried to step in the stall, the horse swung her rear around, blocking him, and tossed her head. "Now, don't go getting your nose all out of joint, pretty girl. We're going to take this slow."

His smooth, soft voice floated through the still night and wrapped around Emma. *Oh, my.* She'd told him to use a calm, soothing voice. Wasn't working. At least not for her. If she got any more hot and bothered she'd end up a puddle on the barn floor.

"You're worried about that baby, aren't you?" Jamie said as he inched closer. The horse stomped her hind foot.

"Watch out. That means she's—"

"I know. She's giving me a warning, aren't you, Trixie girl? You're telling me you mean business. You want me to leave. I hear you, but we need to see that pup you're so intent on protecting." He moved closer. The horse struck out with her hind leg in a quick stroke.

"Be careful. The next step is for her to make that kick count."

"She won't do that." He slid his hand over the animal's neck. "I won't hurt your little one. I promise."

Emma resisted the urge to sigh. If he promised her the moon in that quiet, make-her-melt voice, Emma would check her mailbox expecting to find it in a box with a bright red bow. She swallowed hard. So much for thinking she could treat him like anyone else they helped at the shelter. Her plan had been solid. Unfortunately, her execution stunk. "For a city boy, you're doing a fair job dealing with that horse."

He glanced over his shoulder at her, his eyebrows knit together, a scowl on his handsome face. "What's with all the city-boy comments?"

Simple self-defense.

It reminds me that you won't be around long, and how that's one more reason I shouldn't get any crazy ideas about you and me.

"That bothers you, huh?"

"As if you didn't know." He laughed and continued stroking the horse. The man had killer eyes when they shimmered from his laughter. Eyes that could get a woman to sell her soul for a wooden nickel. "I've been here a lot over the years, and Mick's taught me a thing or two about horses."

"Apparently you were a good student."

"I'm good at a lot of things."

The earth tilted under her as his steamy gaze locked on her, and she knew. He'd take his time with a woman.

Not what she needed to think about right now, but she couldn't stop the images of them together in all kinds of interesting ways and positions from running through her mind. They'd had some great chemistry when they'd dated as teenagers, and she couldn't help but wonder how he'd matured, what he'd learned and how much fun she could have finding out.

Don't say anything. Take the smart route. Ignore the innuendo.

"No quick comeback to put me in my place?"

No way would she touch that statement with a hazmat suit and a ten-foot pole because even that wouldn't be enough protection.

His gaze moved away from hers and focused on the horse. His large hands moved over the animal, soothing and calming. She glanced at the wall over his shoulder, but couldn't shut out his voice. "How about you let us see that baby? You've kind of adopted him, haven't you? I bet you'd make a fine mama. You've got a lot of love to give. I see that in your eyes."

Jamie's words rippled through Emma. What did he see when he looked into her eyes? No, she didn't want to know.

Boots shuffling against concrete sounded Mick's return and snapped her out of her haze.

Still a little unsettled and trying to regroup, Emma turned to the older man. "What took you so long?"

"What did you have to do, make the halter?" Jamie added.

"I had trouble finding the right one." Mick moved past her and handed Jamie the halter.

As Jamie slipped the leather over the horse's head, Mick turned to Emma, his voice low. "How a man treats animals and the way they react to him says a lot about his character."

She nodded. Animals possessed more common sense than most people and didn't let things like money, status and looks cloud their judgment. "They see through the pretense to the real person."

"Nope, you can't fool a horse. Be leery of a man that dogs or horses don't like. They can spot a bad one a mile away." Mick nodded toward his grandson. "He's a good man with a strong heart. A cowboy's heart."

Emma chuckled. The phrase sounded as though it should be an article in *Cowboy Monthly*. Does your man have the heart of a cowboy? Take our survey and find out. "What's that supposed to mean?"

"He loves his family, God and his country. He's honest and tough but has a heart of gold."

She laughed. "You sound like an ad for an old John Wayne movie."

"What are you two talking about?" Jamie asked, his brows scrunched together in confusion. "Remember the puppy? The reason we're out here?"

Mick yawned. "It's past my bedtime, and I've got to be at the restaurant early. If I don't get to sleep I won't be worth a thing. You two have this under control." The older man turned to leave.

"We might need some help," Emma said, afraid of losing her last line of defense.

"Once the two of you get in the stall, unless I hang from the ceiling there won't be room for me." Mick took another step. "Jamie, when I see you at the restaurant tomorrow, let me know how things went."

Then, before she or Jamie could say or do anything, Mick darted for the door. A minute later the barn door creaked open and clanked shut.

"I've never seen him move that fast. It was like someone lit a fire under him," Jamie said, a look of complete confusion plastered on his face.

Wait a minute. Since Mick closed the bar, her grandfather opened in the mornings. Then Mick arrived just before the lunch rush hit. "Something stinks around here and it isn't because the hay needs changing. Mick never opens the restaurant. Why would he say that?"

"I don't know. You want me to go after him?"

"Forget it. You're doing a great job with Trixie. We don't need Mick." The sooner she left, the better, and not just for the pup. She stepped into the stall and stood inside the door as the horse eyed her. "Don't worry, girl. I'm here to help."

Jamie stroked the horse's neck while Emma stepped closer. Impatient to get her hands on the pup, she tried to scoot by the animal. When she did, Trixie swung her rear toward her, knocking Emma off balance. Unable to get her footing and fearing she'd tumble onto the puppy, she grabbed the nearest object to right herself—Jamie. Her hands fisted in his shirt. His arm slid around her waist—warm and strong, offering her support. "Take it easy. There's nothing to worry about."

Was he talking to her or the horse? Not that she cared. Who would when he used that bedroom voice? She tried to focus, but all she could think about was his hand burning her skin through her cotton blouse. That and the fact that he'd been there to catch her.

She'd forgotten how great it felt to have a man's arm around her, but her body remembered. Tingles raced down her spine, bringing heat to places that had been near dead for too long.

Hormone drought. That's what she'd been in, and now that the flow had started again, her body ached. But that's all this was. Her body kicking back into gear. Any man holding her would have brought about the same reaction, the same heat.

Liar.

She'd had relationships since Tucker, probably more than she should have, but hadn't connected with anyone but Clint—but even his touch hadn't lit her up like Jamie's had right now.

This was bad, but being bad could be so good.

"You okay?"

She was fine, all right. Her body was all warm and tingly with happy hormones. A woman could get addicted to feeling like this. All she could do was nod. Her heart beating out a rapid staccato beat, she stepped away.

Trixie shifted nervously and tried to pull away from Jamie. He leaned closer and his soft voice floated over Emma as he started singing. The simple tune, the Beatles' "Blackbird," touched her in a way a song hadn't in years. The man could tame a grizzly when he sang like that. His compassion, his caring wrapped around her. Her heart squeezed.

He's someone special.

No, he's not, and even if he is, I don't care. She had plans. Things she needed to prove to herself and everyone else who'd ever doubted her. A man would only cause problems.

JAMIE SANG TO Trixie TO get himself under control as much as to calm the horse. When Emma had pulled away he'd wanted to drag her back against him. Even after the things they'd said to each other at Halligan's, she still sent his pulse racing. Something that shouldn't happen with such a simple touch.

He was crazy to even think about her after she'd given him clear signals that she wasn't interested. Only a fool kept banging his head against a stone wall, and he was no fool.

Too bad his body had tossed out the memo.

While Trixie settled down quickly, he couldn't say the same thing about himself, especially when Emma scooted past him. Her sweet flowery scent swept over him, keeping his body humming at a fever pitch. No woman should smell that good in a barn. The horse shifted beside him, trying to turn toward Emma to keep an eye on her. "It's okay, sweetheart. Take it easy. You can trust her."

But can I?

When Emma reached the corner, she scooped up the bundle and walked back to him.

"See? I'm not going to hurt him." She held out the pup to the larger animal. "He's fine. Will you take him so I can call Avery?" He took the puppy as Emma placed her call.

Jamie peered at the tiny white puff ball with brown fur around his eyes and on his ears. The tiny thing was all ears and legs.

"We've got the puppy I left the message about. He can't be more than a month old." She moved the dog's lips back to expose his teeth and gums. Then she pinched a section of skin and let it go. "His gums are pretty pale and his skin's taking a while to go back into place. He's probably anemic and dehydrated. He may need fluids."

She paused to listen and turned to him after she ended the call. "Avery will meet me at the shelter."

"Is he going to be okay?"

"I'll be honest. Things can go downhill quickly with puppies this young, but Avery's a great vet. We'll do our best."

"Then we'd better get going." He walked out of the horse stall, the puppy cradled in his large hand.

She dashed after him. "I'll take it from here."

Jamie stopped to wait for her and glanced at his watch. "It's after eleven. What kind of man would I be if I let you go out alone at this late hour? I'd never forgive myself if something happened to you. Plus, I'm kind of attached to this guy." He paused and turned the puppy upside down. "Yup. It's a he."

When she opened her mouth to argue, he said, "We can either stand here arguing, and you won't win, by the way, or we can get this puppy the help he needs."

"You're going to be stubborn about this, aren't you?" He stared at her. She sighed. "Let's go."

WHEN EMMA AND JAMIE reached the Estes Park animal shelter parking lot, the glimmer from the lone street light and the crescent moon sprinkled the area.

She unlocked the shelter's front door, entered and turned on the lights. "Follow me. We'll clean him up while we're waiting for Avery. We need to get the fleas off him. They can be deadly for a dog this young."

"This guy's had a tough start." Jamie scratched the pup behind the ear as she led him through the shelter to a back room. "It'll get better from here, buddy."

Emma told him to hold the dog over the tub. Once he did, she grabbed the spray nozzle, turned on the tap and waited for the water to warm up.

"How does someone with a music degree and a band end up working as the volunteer coordinator for a local animal shelter?"

Such a simple question. Small talk, really. The kind strangers at a party tossed out to each other without even thinking. How could something so supposedly inconsequential pack such a wallop?

"It's a long story."

"I've got plenty of time."

Everyone in town knew her story, but no one ever asked her to talk about what she'd gone through. They just knew, but they didn't understand. She considered fobbing him off with some vague "life happens" flip comment, but something stopped her. His eyes. They could get a woman to reveal her deepest secrets.

He's got a cowboy's heart.

Jamie would understand, and right now she wanted that. Needed it.

"After I graduated from college I moved to Nashville again." She'd packed up her hopes and dreams, tossed them in a 2003 Camry with one hundred and twenty thousand miles on it and swore the second time things would be different. "I was in a band and things were going well. Really well. We'd caught the eye of a promoter and he was on the verge of taking us on. Then my mom was diagnosed with pancreatic cancer."

"Cancer's always bad, but that one's brutal."

She nodded. The odds had been against her mom. Only a little over 20 percent of people diagnosed with the disease were alive after one year, but Emma had hoped her mom would be one of the lucky ones. "Between chemo and the cancer she felt pretty lousy most of the time. She was weak and in so much pain. I came home to help with her care."

Emma held her hand under the spray of water to test the temperature, gently wet the pup's white fluffy fur and squirted soap over him, as memories welled up inside her.

As her mother's health had continued to deteriorate, Emma couldn't leave. She was needed, but more important, she wanted to spend as much time as she could with her mother. While she didn't regret her decision, dealing with the endless appointments and medical issues had drained her emotionally. She'd needed something else to occupy her mind. Something to feed her soul. She'd needed somewhere to regroup. Or to fall apart.

"Once I realized I was going to stay longer than I planned, I told the band I wouldn't be coming back. Turned out they'd already replaced me. They just forgot to tell me."

"Real nice of them. They could've at least had the balls to tell you."

"That's what I said. Anyway, that's when I decided I needed a place of my own. Staying at my parents' house was—" She paused and chewed on her lower lip.

"Too much to take, almost overwhelming."

She nodded, stunned at how he'd understood what she couldn't put into words. "To get an apartment I needed to support myself. I thought about teaching music in a school, but those jobs are hard to come by in a small community. People get one and keep it until they retire."

After she massaged the soap through the puppy's fur to dislodge as many fleas as possible, she rinsed the dog. Small dark specks floated among the soap bubbles. "Those black things are fleas."

Jamie stared into the sink. "Poor fella. It's a wonder he's got any blood left with those things gnawing at him."

She reached into the cabinet above the sink and pulled out a fine-tooth comb. "This should get any critters that held on and survived the bath."

"So you couldn't find a teaching position?" Jamie asked, returning to their previous conversation.

"No. I considered giving private lessons, but that takes time to find enough students to pay the bills."

"And I suppose you were stubbornly attached to luxuries like hot water, electricity and food."

His comment made her smile. She liked how he made her do that. "Call me crazy. So when I heard the shelter needed a volunteer coordinator, I thought, I love animals and this could be a way for me to pay the bills while I help take care of Mom. It's not what I want to do forever, but don't get me wrong. I don't regret my decision. Mom died eight months after her diagnosis."

"Living with no regrets is worth a lot."

Too bad she couldn't say the same for other areas of her life. At least she was working on her career regrets.

The puppy whimpered when the comb stuck in his tangled fur. "Hang on, pal," Jamie said as he scratched it behind the ears. "I know you feel lousy right now, but things are gonna get better from here."

Good-looking. A voice that could melt the hardest woman's heart, and he took care of kids and small defenseless animals.

Where was Avery? She could really use the cavalry showing up. A girl could only hold out for so long.

Chapter Eight

"I see you're taking care of the fleas," Avery said when she walked into the room, and Emma almost sighed in relief. Much longer and her self-control would've disintegrated like a child's snowman on an unseasonably warm winter day.

After Avery introduced herself she moved around the room opening drawers and cupboards, collecting the supplies she needed to treat the puppy's issues.

"You're going to need all this for him?" Jamie said as he stared at the materials spread out on the table. "This has to be expensive."

"It's not easy balancing animals' needs with our donations." Avery filled a syringe with saline and delivered the liquid to the puppy under his skin. As she squirted another liquid into the animal's mouth to deal with any internal parasites, she glanced at Emma, her eyebrows raised, and nodded slightly toward Jamie as if to say, *Here's our opening to ask him about the fundraiser. Go for it.*

Time for her, as the perfect employee, to put her money where her mouth was. "Speaking of donations, we've got our major fund-raiser coming up. Avery and I were talking about a way you could help us."

"We're having a Pet Walk at Stanley Park. Last year

we added Emma's band giving a concert to the event," Avery said. "Since you've created such uproar online, we wondered if you'd sing with Emma's band at the event."

He laughed, as if he thought they were joking. When Emma and Avery didn't join in, he froze and stared at them. "Don't tell me you're serious."

They both nodded. The guy really didn't have a clue how amazing his voice was? That seemed hard to believe.

"You think my singing will help the shelter raise money? I can't believe anyone would buy a ticket for that."

"Obviously you haven't seen the online video of you at Halligan's or read any of the comments on Facebook." Or looked in a mirror. Women would come out in droves to watch him stand onstage and read *War and Peace*.

He shook his head. "I've been enjoying being unplugged since I got to Colorado."

"Then let me fill you in," Emma said. "I swear half of the single women I know who saw the video today contacted me. They wanted to know if you're available and how they can meet you."

"You're kidding." A blush crept up from his neck into his face.

"She's not," Avery said.

"As long as you're sure. Singing with the band sounds like fun."

For one of us, maybe.

"Fantastic. I'll let you two work out the details about the performance while I see to publicity. Now back to this little guy." Avery patted the puppy. "We'll put out the word about our friend tomorrow. Hopefully we can reunite him with his mom, but we need to figure out what to do with him tonight. He'll need to be fed every two hours. I hate to call any of our volunteers this late. Can you take him, Emma?"

"My apartment doesn't take pets, remember?"

Jamie stared at her. "Isn't that like an atheist working at a church?"

"Ha-ha. That's a good one. It was the only affordable place I could find with an opening. What about you, Avery?"

"If I bring home any more animals Reed is going to make me sleep on the couch. We've got Baxter, and we're watching Thor for Jess. In addition we're fostering Molly the Doberman mix and Mumford the ninety-pound Lab. The apartment is overflowing with dogs. I don't dare bring home a puppy that needs feeding every two hours. You sure you can't take him for the night, Em?"

"With Arlene Rogers living next door? That woman has Vulcan hearing, and after the last time I got caught bringing my work home, so to speak, my landlord threatened to evict me."

"I'll take him," Jamie said. He turned to Emma. "That is, if you'll help me get him settled in and show me what to do."

She tried to think of a reason to say no and then thought, what was the point? The saying "she'd be closing the barn door after the horses had already escaped" popped into her head. "Since I have to take you back to the ranch anyway, I might as well stick around to help with the first feeding." The calm and steady tone of her voice, despite the knot in her stomach, surprised her.

Something told her she'd be smarter pressing her luck with the landlord than spending any more time with Jamie. The things she did for her day job.

FIFTEEN MINUTES LATER, when Jamie and Emma stood in Mick's small outdated kitchen, Jamie almost smiled at Emma's determination to stay all business with him. If he moved closer to her, she backpedaled. She failed to make eye contact. Her voice remained devoid of emotion. As she explained what he'd need to do to care for the pup through the night, the harder she tried to remain detached, the more intrigued he became. She was just trying too hard to put him in his place, to show him he couldn't get under her skin. That had to mean something, didn't it?

He dug into a drawer, found a can opener and handed it to Emma. While she opened the can of puppy milk replacer and filled the dropper, she explained that every two hours he'd feed the liquid a little bit at a time to the pup.

When she went to hand him the dropper, he picked up the carrier containing the puppy and headed for the living room instead. He looked at her over his shoulder. "I don't know about you, but I've got to sit down before I fall down."

"It's been a long night, hasn't it?" she said as she followed him.

He nodded toward the pictures scattered around the living room. "I love this house. It's the kind of home that should be filled with family and friends. Looks like it used to be that kind of place."

"Before Mick's wife died they entertained all the time. My grandpa G says Mick's been so lonely since Carol died. You coming into his life has been a blessing."

"It's been that for me, too." A calm port in the storm his life had become. After he and Emma settled onto the worn brown couch, Jamie retrieved the puppy. Wide sleepy eyes peered up at him as he accepted the dropper from Emma. He squeezed some milk into the puppy's mouth. "He's a cute little guy. He won't have any problem getting adopted if we can't find his mom, will he?"

"He shouldn't have any problem finding a home."

"I always wanted a dog."

"How come you never had one?"

For a few days he had. In fourth grade he'd written a persuasive paper on why his parents should let him have a dog. He smiled thinking of his arguments. He'd get more exercise walking the dog and play fewer video games. Having a pet would teach him responsibility. People who had pets were healthier because petting a dog lowered a person's blood pressure. He'd shown his parents his paper. They'd knuckled and had taken him to the local shelter.

He'd been so excited when they'd brought Rocco home. He'd crawled out of bed a half an hour early to walk him before school every day and then walked him again first thing when he got home. They'd been inseparable, the pup even sleeping on the foot of his bed at night.

"My sister had asthma so we couldn't have a dog."

Of course they hadn't known that until his sister had suffered a severe attack, ending up in the emergency room the third night they'd had Rocco. The first thing the E.R. doctor said was having a dog in the house would make Rachel's condition worse. The next day they gave Rocco to a couple across town, and Jamie cried himself to sleep for a week.

When he graduated from college he'd considered getting a dog, but the time never seemed right. He'd been focused on his career and didn't feel it would be fair to the animal to bring him into a home where he'd spend so much time alone.

"You have a sister? Is she older or younger?"

"I have two, actually. My oldest sister is only a year younger than I am. My parents tried for seven years to get pregnant and went through all kinds of fertility treatments before they adopted me. Then, boom. They got pregnant with my sister. Three years after that they had my other sister."

"Was that hard, being the only one adopted?"

No one had ever come right out and asked him that before. People hinted at the subject and hoped he'd indulge their curiosity, but he'd always ignored the implied question. For the first time he wanted to tell someone what it had felt like. No, not someone. He wanted to share what it had been like with Emma. "Everyone in my family is very analytical. Very left-brained. I'm the opposite."

Emma nodded, and understanding flared in her soft gaze. "I'm the only girl in my family. All my brothers are outdoor types, and two of them are ranchers like my father. The farthest any of them has ventured is to the other side of town when they purchased their own spread. You know the Sesame Street song that goes 'one of these things is not like the other'? That was my theme song."

So that's why she understood. He'd never have guessed she was the odd one out in her family, too. She seemed so confident, so at ease in the world, but then people probably said the same about him.

"Noncreative types find people like us hard to understand. Sometimes it was like I was speaking a different language."

He started to deny what she'd said, even though he'd

thought it more than once, but stopped himself. Looking into Emma's expressive face, he knew she wouldn't judge him as being disrespectful to the couple who loved him when the woman who gave birth to him refused to. "I know what you mean. My parents were supportive. They went to all my orchestra events. They volunteered at school and in Cub Scouts. They are great parents, but it was weird at times. My sisters would do something that reminded them of someone in the family." He stopped. *And I didn't have that genetic link.*

"And you didn't have that connection," Emma said, summing up his sentiments. "Is that what made you search for your birth family?"

Would he have been so anxious to find where he'd come from if his siblings had been adopted, too, or if he'd been an only child? Would he have been more content? "The genetic link my sisters shared, the fact that people saw bits and pieces of our parents or other relatives in them, made me think about who I was. I wondered what part of me was because of my DNA and what came from the people who raised me."

What it came down to was control. What he had the ability to change about himself and what was his genetic blueprint. He glanced at the puppy who'd fallen asleep curled up on his lap now that his belly was full. He lifted the animal and placed him inside the carrier on an old towel they'd put inside.

"When I met Mick, so many things made sense. Like where my musical talent and my ability with numbers came from." He smiled thinking of his grandfather. "Mick's amazing with numbers, too. He knows what his costs are for everything, salaries, overhead, utilities, food. What his profit margins are. Once I understood what came from him, I could appreciate everything my parents did for me more. What I am because they raised me."

The dim light of the table lamp bounced off the tears in Emma's eyes. He reached out and placed his hand over hers. "I'm sorry. I shouldn't have said anything. I didn't mean to upset you."

"It's not your fault. I asked you because I wanted to know."

All those years ago, he'd felt an instant connection with Emma, but he hadn't appreciated the fact. Now, after all the women that had come and gone in his life, he knew what a rare thing they shared. The question was now that he was older and wiser, what should he do about it?

LISTENING TO JAMIE, Emma wondered if she was getting a glimpse into her son's future. Would some of the same uncertainties and questions that plagued Jamie haunt her son? But unlike Jamie's birth mother, she wouldn't turn her son away if he knocked on her door. She'd hug the stuffing out of him and get down on her knees to thank God for sending him back into her life.

"What did you decide to do about contacting the people who adopted your son?"

"I called the agency and told them if the parents expressed any interest in talking to me, I'm open to that. Right now I don't think doing more than that is good for anyone."

"Did you ever consider keeping the baby?"

Emma stared at Jamie, trying to decide if she should tell him the truth, something she'd never told anyone. Her chest tightened and she knew. Now was the time, here in the quiet stillness with this man, to let go of some of the pain she'd carried for far too long. Resentment that she thought she'd let go of.

"I did. That was why I came home when the baby's father and I broke up."

"Where had you been living?"

His question caught her off guard. She kept forgetting he didn't know all the details. She explained how she and Tucker had left for Nashville soon after Jamie had returned to Juilliard that summer.

She'd been lonely when Jamie had left and nervous about going to college. Then Tucker had dumped Monica and told her he wanted to get back together. He'd been so apologetic and full of dreams. He'd told her they could have a career together in country music, and she'd been naive enough to believe him.

"When things fell apart, I came home. I needed my parents' guidance and support."

She'd received the advice, that was for sure. She could almost remember her mother's lecture verbatim all these years later. Some words never left a person.

If you decide to keep this baby, you can't live here. Your father and I won't help you financially. You'll have to earn enough to pay for your living expenses and for day care. We're not going to keep your child all day while you work. Think of what life would be like. Is that really what you want for your child?

"Did they help you?"

"They felt my giving the baby up for adoption was the best solution." Who was she kidding? They thought it was the only solution. "They said if I kept my child I'd have to support myself. They wouldn't help with money or day care."

"That seems harsh."

At first his comment surprised her, but then his

words worked their way inside her, making her take another look at what had happened. At the time she'd told herself their tough-love approach had helped her grow up and face reality, but had they needed to be so cold? So judgmental? She'd been a good kid, who'd never caused them trouble. She was an honor student who, unlike her brothers, never drank or did drugs in high school. Her parents never had to remind her to do her chores. She'd been the model child.

Until she'd gotten pregnant, and even then, she'd been acting responsibly. She'd been on the pill and had taken it faithfully. She was just one of the unlucky 8 percent.

Her mother's words rang in her ears. *People will think we didn't raise you right. That we were bad parents.* And her father had just sat there.

They'd never really supported her career, and when she'd come home feeling like a failure, they'd reinforced that. *We knew nothing good would come of your going to Nashville.*

"There were options between financially supporting you and not helping at all," Jamie said, pulling her away from her memories.

He was right. There were. Unless you were more concerned with what your neighbors thought than your child. Part of why they'd wanted her to give her child up had been because then they could pretend she was still that perfect child. "I never thought of that before."

Her mother had been so unbending, so unwilling to try to understand, but when she'd gotten sick, who had she called? Her daughter. "I need you to come home. There are things I can't do for myself. I need another woman here to help me."

And what had Emma done? She'd put her life on

hold and rushed home to help a woman who'd never supported her dreams.

What did any of that matter now? She couldn't change the past. "They wanted to make sure I considered what raising a child entailed. At nineteen, with nothing but a high school education, what kind of life could I give a child? If they'd bailed me out financially when things got tough or provided day care I might have made a different decision. It would have been so easy to be selfish."

"What about the baby's father?"

"He made it clear he didn't want anything to do with fatherhood." *Or me.* "He didn't have any money then either, so he couldn't help financially. He was living in Nashville, playing small clubs for dinner and drinks." At least until he'd gotten the recording contract with her revamped song, but it had taken years for him to move to easy street.

"You're amazing. What you did couldn't have been easy."

"That's why it was great seeing the other side of the story. The Sandbergs showed me the joy in adoption. You have, too."

Lord, she and Jamie had gotten maudlin tonight. Needing to turn the conversation to a topic lighter than a semitruck, she said, "The band's rehearsing tomorrow night. If you want, you could join us to run through a few songs for the Pet Walk concert." She nibbled on her lower lip for a minute, trying to decide if she should plunge ahead. What the hell. Why not? "I've been thinking about Henry's suggestion that you should replace Molly in the band."

She paused, hoping he'd jump in with a quick "sure, I'd like to do that" and save her from having to ask.

When she sneaked a peek at him, he leaned back in the chair and crossed his arms over his chest. Nope, he had no intention of making this easy for her.

"I might have been a little hasty dismissing the idea. At the bar the other night you sounded like you might be open to the possibility." Another quick peek. Nothing. He sat there as stiff and still as the Rocky Mountains. "I've spoken with Luke and Grayson, my bass player and drummer. They think the suggestion has merit. I watched a video of you on YouTube playing with the symphony. You're incredible."

His smile and the light in his eyes disappeared. She didn't know what she'd done, but she'd somehow hurt him.

"Before you go any further, I have to tell you something. I hurt my hand a few months ago. I had surgery to repair the tendon damage, but I've had dexterity problems since then."

"How bad is it?"

"The Philharmonic let me go."

Her vow to remain detached hit the floor and shattered as she gazed into his anguish-filled eyes. She knew all too well what it felt like to be dumped. To see the dreams she'd worked so hard to achieve splinter before her eyes like delicate crystal on cement, and to feel the helplessness of being unable to stop the destruction.

It sucked big-time, no matter what the cause.

"I've been there, for a different reason, but there's nothing I can say that would make you feel better or doesn't sound lame."

"You're the first person that's been honest. Everyone else thinks they can fix it, wants to offer me career counseling or thinks I'm on the verge of suicide."

She nodded. "It gets old."

"You got that right. I came here to get away from all the well-meaning advice. I have a whole new understanding of the phrase 'killing someone with kindness.'" He flashed a weak smile, but what got to her was the trust shining in his eyes. "Mick's the only one who knows."

Until you.

Warning bells clanged in her head, drowning out everything else. She didn't want to share confidences with him.

Too late. Even before now. Don't you remember what you shared earlier in the barn?

Okay, so she didn't want to share any *more* confidences with him. Doing that made it too difficult to keep things light and easy with a guy.

"What are your plans—" She couldn't bring herself to finish her question. *If you can't return to the symphony.*

"You mean if I can't play well enough for the symphony?"

She nodded.

This was scary. They'd started finishing each other's sentences.

"The hell if I know. I was lousy at everything but music and math in school, but doing anything mathwise would mean going back to college and starting over. Who am I kidding? No matter what else I do, I'll be starting over." He rubbed the back of his neck. "The hard work around the ranch and at the bar has strengthened my hand, but I don't know if it'll ever improve enough for me to return to the symphony."

For the first time since she'd picked him up at the airport, weariness lined his face. That and something deeper. Fear? *He's scared because he doesn't know what to do with his life.*

She thought about listing all the options people had mentioned to her when she'd come home the last time. He could teach in the school system and privately. He could write music, but she remembered how all of those suggestions had left her feeling—hollow. And Jamie craved the performing as she did. It was part of him.

"I miss playing music." His words tore at her heart.

She really should tell him to forget about playing with the band. She should say they could rehearse the songs for him to sing at the fund-raiser and leave things there. That was the common-sense decision, but she knew what he was going through, how it felt to try to recover from a setback like this. How overpowering the fear of losing the dream he'd built his life around could be.

But if he couldn't play well enough for the Philharmonic, what were the chances he could handle their music?

Come on, you don't need Charlie Daniels on the fiddle. Give Jamie a chance.

How many guys did she know who would've tossed their pride aside by coming clean even though it was the decent thing to do?

"If you want to try playing with the band and see how things go, I'm willing to give it a shot. Why don't you bring your fiddle tomorrow?"

So much for common sense.

"I'd like that. Now, how about having dinner with me after rehearsal?"

Sirens clanged in her head again. Red lights flashed. "I don't date musicians."

"Any particular reason why?"

"They're self-centered and about as reliable as a fortune-teller."

"That's an awfully broad brush you're using there."

"I'm just going on past experience."

"Some men might see what you said as a challenge to prove you wrong."

Determination darkened his eyes to the color of strong coffee, and she knew he was on the verge of being one of those guys. She froze, unable to catch her breath. For the briefest second she thought about what it would be like to have a man like Jamie want her. A good, solid man. An honest man.

Consuming, but a true give-and-take. That's what it would be like. Jamie could so easily throw her life out of whack.

When he leaned closer, everything else faded away. His presence overwhelmed her more than it had in the barn, but in an oh-so-good, I-feel-like-a-woman way. Heat flashed through her as if she was made of October grass, scorching her, leaving her aching, and he hadn't even touched her.

She stared into his eyes and realized he had the longest eyelashes she'd ever seen. That wasn't fair when he was already so handsome. His eyes had always mesmerized her. Even at nineteen there had been something in his gaze, a look that said he understood things most guys his age failed to.

Sitting here with Jamie in the dim light from the old lamp perched on the scratched end table, she wanted to believe he was different, even though common sense said the odds were lousy. She should move away from him. Say something. Break the spell. She knew what she should do, but she couldn't force her body to move. Truth be told, she didn't want to.

He reached out and cupped her face. His thumb brushed over her lips and she resisted the urge to run her tongue over his skin and taste him.

Then his lips covered hers.

Chapter Nine

Emma melted into Jamie, letting his strong presence shut out everything else but the heat racing through her. His lips, warm and inviting, teased hers. Her hands clung to his shoulders, needing his solid strength as awareness rippled through her. She'd missed this. Being held by a man. Connecting with a human being on this intimate level.

Her tongue slipped between his lips to tease his. His strong arms wrapped around her, pulling her even closer. Her hands fisted in his shirt, holding on to him as though he was her only anchor as the emotions, passion and need crashed over her.

"Whoever he was, he must've been a real dick to put that much hurt in your eyes. We're not all cut from the same cloth. Let me prove I'm not like him."

Reality kicked her hard in the teeth. She went to pull away from him, and realized she was on his lap, practically straddling him. How had that happened? She'd been so far gone and she hadn't even realized. With as much dignity as she could muster with the evidence of his desire pressing against her hip, she slipped off his lap and slid away from him.

She wanted to give Jamie a chance. Wanted to believe he could be different. That he was someone who'd put her first. He looked and sounded so sincere, but how could she trust her instincts when she'd been wrong before? Dogs and horses were good judges of character, but she couldn't tell a good man from a hole in the ground.

No more. She'd learned her lesson. She jumped off the couch, grabbed her purse and clutched it to her chest like a shield. "You know what to do."

He flashed her a you-bet-I-do smile.

Her heart tripped. Boy, did he know what to do. He'd demonstrated that emphatically. She cleared her throat. "You know *what to do for the puppy* tonight. Drop him off when we open tomorrow morning at ten."

Then she ran for the front door without looking back.

Once in her car, she locked the doors and leaned her forehead against the steering wheel. Her heart beat out a staccato tempo while her body coursed with need. Since coming home she'd worked so hard to control her emotions, to keep from letting anything get to her. She'd decided no more relying on her heart to make decisions. That's where she'd gone wrong so many times in her life. A heart that had been broken couldn't be trusted. She'd rely on her head and her gut instead.

Nothing would sidetrack her this time. Not when she had her life back on course, a plan in place and her goal in sight. She'd get the band ready for the state fair competition, win said contest, impress Phillip Brandise in the consultation audition and land a recording contract.

Kissing Jamie was nowhere in her plans.

Fool me once, shame on you. Fool me twice, shame on me. Fool me three times, and I should be locked up for my own protection.

MONDAY MORNING EMMA walked into the shelter thankful that her weekend was over. Talk about a mess. But now she could focus on work. She intended to forget about Jamie, his soul-searching eyes and his melt-her-panties kisses.

Her plan lasted for all of twenty minutes. Right up until the volunteers and the rest of the shelter staff arrived. After that a constant parade of people tromped through her office to bombard her with questions.

What was Jamie like? How long was he staying in town? Did he have a girlfriend back East? Was he as *wonderful* as he seemed from the way he acted onstage? Could she introduce them? After an hour of endless questions and listening to every female in the place between the age of sixteen and eighty ooh and aah over Jamie, Emma reached the limit of her patience.

"And my nightmare weekend has followed me into the office," Emma said when she sought refuge in Avery's office. After closing the door behind her, she plopped into the chair in front of her friend's desk. "I know this is a small town, but you'd think someone else must have done something over the weekend that people could gossip about. How about I pay you to create a scandal or do something foolish? Nothing major, mind you. Just give everyone something other than Jamie Westland to talk about. By the way, if our volunteers are any indication, what you've done to publicize him singing at the Pet Walk concert is working. And to make matters worse, Shirley's here today. She's a wonderful volunteer and a generous donor, but she's about to drive me completely insane pumping me for information about Jamie, who she *swears* is the perfect man for Shay because they have singing in common. If you don't do something to get everyone to quit hounding me about him, I won't be responsible for my actions."

Emma paused, realizing she was out of breath. When

the silence continued, she glanced at Avery, who sat behind her desk, hands splayed across the smooth wooden surface, a glazed look in her eyes. "Say something, Avery."

"I'm just trying to figure out who you are and what you've done with my calm, levelheaded, never-loses-patience friend."

"Okay. So I've gone off the deep end a little." At Avery's raised eyebrow, Emma said, "Okay, so I've gone off the deep end a lot, but help me out. Let me hide out here until Shirley's shift is over."

"This isn't about what's going on here at the shelter. You can handle everyone's questions and comments about Jamie with a smart quip or a clever change of subject. What's really bothering you? Did something happen last night between you two?"

"What makes you think anything—" Emma rubbed her throbbing temples. "Forget it. Even at my best I couldn't pull off that lie, and I'm not anywhere near my best. He kissed me, but that's not the worst part. I kissed him back."

I nearly crawled into his hip pocket.

"So what's the problem?"

"I liked it. Way too much."

"I'm still waiting for the problem part."

"Now is the worst time for me to get involved with someone, and I'm such a lousy judge of character when it comes to guys. Remember Clint? The guy who replaced me in my previous band two weeks after I came home to take care of Mom, even though he promised he wouldn't?"

Of course that's not what he'd told her. Instead every time she'd talked with him, he'd said he couldn't wait for her to come back. He missed her. The band wasn't the same without her.

He'd told her what she'd wanted to hear.

"Then there's the fact that my relationships have a way of breaking up my bands. Do I really need to go on?"

"As my mother would say, quit borrowing trouble. If you want my advice, I say have some fun and don't worry about the future so much."

"Borrowing trouble? I think trouble has camped out on my front step."

JAMIE DROVE ACROSS town to the Estes Park animal shelter, the puppy he'd started calling Trooper curled up asleep in the carrier on the passenger seat. Last night with Emma had been eye-opening in a whole lot of ways.

He'd shared things with her he'd never told anyone. Never really wanted to. When he'd talked about his family, she'd understood how he'd felt both a part of and somehow separate from everyone else.

Then she'd surprised him by asking him to play in the band.

Everything had been perfect until he kissed her.

Damn the guy who'd made her so skittish. When he'd held her and her fingers teased the sensitive spot behind his ear as he kissed her, he'd forgotten everything, his hand and whether or not he'd ever play like he once had. About what he'd do with his life if he couldn't return to the symphony. All he'd thought about was Emma and how she made him feel. As though there was more to life than music and his career. As though he belonged. With her. How he wanted to spend time with her.

Time. How long would he be here? He hadn't given

much thought to it. He flexed his hand. In the short time
he'd been here, the physical work around the ranch and
at the restaurant combined with his exercises seemed
to be helping his hand, bolstering his hope that his life
could return to normal.

But what about Emma? Was it fair to her to start a
relationship when he wouldn't be sticking around? He
shook himself mentally. Talk about jumping the gun.
All they'd done was share a kiss. Granted, one that had
nearly melted his socks, but it was just one.

As he pulled into the shelter parking lot, he told himself he was being silly. How long he intended to stay
didn't make any difference, especially since he hadn't
made a secret of the fact that he planned on returning
to New York. Plus, when did anyone get a guarantee
on how much time they had together?

Dating was always a crapshoot.

Confident now that he had sorted things out, he
parked Mick's truck, picked up the carrier and headed
for the front door. Unlike last night, when he entered
the shelter lobby today the place hummed with activity.
Meows and barking echoed through the small space.
The sound of ringing phones and the buzz of printers
floated through the air, mixing with snippets of conversation.

The pretty blonde with big brown eyes behind the
desk greeted him with a huge smile. "Hi, Jamie. I'm
Callie. You were fantastic at Halligan's Friday night.
I was there with some friends. I can't wait to hear you
sing again at the shelter benefit. I've already got my
ticket. Maybe I'll camp out so I can be in the front row."

"Take a breath, girl, before the man's ear falls off
from all that chatter," said an older gray-haired woman
dressed in a T-shirt with the phrase Love Me, Love My

Cat across her ample bosom. Then she introduced herself as Shirley. "I might have to come hear you sing myself. You've been the big talk around town."

He flashed a smile in Shirley's direction as he placed the pet carrier on the counter. The fact that people were paying good money to hear him sing unsettled him more than he expected. Singing karaoke was one thing, but a paid performance? Despite what Emma and Avery said, he hadn't really believed anyone would buy tickets because of him. Maybe he should've thought the offer through more before he'd said yes. "Thanks for buying a ticket. I'm glad I can help out the shelter."

"Are you taking song requests?" Callie asked, batting her eyes at him. She was pretty enough and curvy in all the right places, but her predatory gleam left him feeling like the mouse just before the cat pounced on him.

"I haven't even thought about it, but that's not a bad idea." Especially considering he didn't have a clue what songs would be good for his voice and something the audience wanted to hear.

"You're the spitting image of Mick when he was younger, except for the hairstyle," Shirley said. "Now I understand why you've been all my granddaughter Shay can talk about. You're one fine-looking fella."

Her comment caught him off guard. He tried not to show it, but knew he'd failed. Lord, he hadn't felt this awkward around women since he was thirteen. "I'm looking for Emma."

"I haven't seen her this morning. Now, about your concert." Callie leaned toward him and wet her lips. "Do you know any Luke Bryan songs? I love the song 'Drunk on You.' You know, if your hair was a bit shorter you could be his twin. Not that I don't like your hair."

"Dial it back, missy. It's unseemly of you to act so

forward." Shirley grabbed a scrap of paper and a pencil off the desk, jotted something down and handed the note to him. "If you want to see the town, give my granddaughter a call."

"You thought I was too forward?" Callie said.

Fans of the Philharmonic never acted like this. The most they did was write a polite email extolling his skills and the emotions his playing evoked in words that usually sent him running for the dictionary. "If you tell me where Emma's office is, I'll be on my way."

He wanted to get out of there before they started tugging at him like a turkey wishbone on Thanksgiving Day.

"It's the one to the left at the end of that hallway." Shirley pointed the way. "You think about calling Shay."

Anxious to escape, he thanked the woman, picked up Trooper's carrier and headed for the hallway. After a few steps, Emma's voice drifted toward him. "Forget about having Jamie sing at the fund-raiser. What we should ask him to do is let us raffle off a date with him. That's what'll bring in big bucks. Maybe then everyone will leave me alone and quit asking me to fix them up with him."

He knocked on the door and stepped inside the office. Avery laughed seeing him, while Emma blushed bright pink. He couldn't resist teasing her. "Raffle off a date? That's an interesting idea, but what's in it for me?"

Emma groaned. "Talk about awkward. How do I keep putting my foot in my mouth whenever you're around?"

"I guess I bring out the best in you."

"I was kidding about the raffle. It's been a long morning," she continued.

"Let's not dismiss the idea so quickly. It could make a lot—"

"Not unless you rig it so that one of you two is the winner," he said before Avery could finish. "After the way the women acted when I was onstage the other night and hearing Callie and Shirley go around out there, I'm a little scared of the women in town."

"Callie and Shirley are working the desk together? We never schedule them at the same time."

"I can see why."

Emma covered her eyes with her hands, but peered at him through her fingers. "Do I want to know what happened?"

He gave her and Avery a quick rundown of the gauntlet he'd been forced to run. "For a while there I was worried a fight would break out."

"As the director of the shelter, let me apologize for my volunteers," Avery said in all seriousness.

Emma groaned and reached for a pencil and a Post-it note off the desk. As she started writing, she said, "I'm making a note to discuss that we're not a dating service with the volunteers."

"I don't know," Jamie said. "You might be missing out on a way to up your adoption numbers. Adopt a pet and get a date for Friday night."

Emma laughed. "That's a good one. Thanks. I needed a laugh. It could be our new holiday slogan."

"It's good to see your sense of humor is returning. You had me worried for a while there." Avery nodded toward the carrier in Jamie's hand. "How's our little friend doing?"

"Trooper—that's what I started calling him—is more active and alert this morning. Have you had any luck finding his mother?"

"Not yet, but we're still looking. Have we found someone to foster him?" Emma turned toward Avery, who shook her head.

"If you haven't, I can keep him a while longer."

"I'll let you two talk about that while I give this little guy a look-over since he's here." Avery stood, picked up the carrier and left, shutting the door behind her.

Emma nodded to the chair beside her. "If you're willing to keep him, that would be great. If you give me your phone number I'll call you when we find someone to foster him."

"That's a slick way to ask a guy for his number."

"I don't think there's anything else for us to discuss," Emma said in what he now recognized was her best all-business voice. "You're more than welcome to sit here until Avery's finished examining Trooper. Now, if you'll excuse me, I have to give Callie and Shirley a quick how-to-work-the-front-desk refresher course."

LATER THAT EVENING when Emma walked into her father's garage, the one he'd been kind enough to clear out when she'd started the band, she still couldn't believe how she'd let Jamie get to her at the shelter. He'd been so determined to push her buttons.

That's a slick way to ask a guy for his number.

And what had she come back with? Pretty much nothing but a lame excuse that she had work duties to see to. His laughter taunting her when she'd left Avery's office told her he'd known she was taking the coward's way out.

Damn right she had. Sometimes retreating was the only way to survive the battle.

"I talked to Jamie," Emma said when Luke and Grayson arrived. "He's bringing his fiddle with him when he comes to work on the songs for the Pet Walk concert."

She'd debated whether or not to tell them about Jamie's hand, but decided it wasn't her place to share the news. Could be that everything would go fine when he played with them and no one would need to know anything about his injury.

But more important, she kept remembering the trust shining in his eyes last night when he'd told her how he'd come to Estes Park to get away. She couldn't betray him.

"I checked out the video of you two singing. Man, women go crazy over that guy. Some of their comments online made me blush."

"Sure, he's got a great voice, but what's he got that we don't have?" Luke nodded toward Grayson.

Seriously? How could men be so clueless? While Luke and Grayson were good-looking and in shape, they weren't...well, Jamie. They lacked his charisma, his charm. That rare "it" so few people possessed.

"He could bring a whole new demographic to the Pet Walk," Luke said.

"Single, man-hungry women?" Emma shuddered at the thought of every woman within a thirty-mile radius showing up at the event. Wouldn't that be a fun audience to perform in front of?

Visions of screaming single women in their audience all vying for Jamie's attention danced in her head. That's what she'd always dreamed of her concerts being—wild events with women tossing their lace thongs onstage. That would get everyone to take them seriously.

What had she done?

"That's my favorite demographic—women between

eighteen and twenty-five," Luke said, a big asinine smile on his face.

"This could be way more fun than last year," Grayson added.

Maybe for the rest of the band.

"Jamie's already helping increase our visibility," Luke said. "Because you're in the video with him, people are checking out our stuff, too, and the likes on our videos are way up. We need to capitalize on this."

"I was amazed how good you two sounded."

Here we go. Same song, second verse. The old insecurity welled up inside her, reminding her of the comments she'd heard when she'd returned to Nashville and started singing without Tucker. *Your guitar skills are amazing as always, and your voice sounds great, but you're not at the level you were when you and Tucker sang together. Have you thought about joining another band or finding another singing partner?*

The first time she'd heard that after a show she'd brushed the statement off, but when that became the standard response from industry professionals, she realized a solo career wouldn't get her where she wanted to be.

"The heat you two generated lit up the stage. I've never heard you sound like that," Luke said.

Ouch. Hearing it from half the town had been bad enough, but hearing it from one of her bandmates, who knew her ability probably better than she did and whose judgment she valued, shook her.

"Are you saying I sounded like crap before?"

"Man, you're touchy today. You know that's not what I meant," Luke said.

Forget about it. Don't doubt yourself or doubt what you're meant to do with your life. Instead, think of sing-

*ing with Jamie as the means to achieving your ends—a
recording contract.* If he could help her and the band
win the state fair contest, did anything else matter?

But then the little nagging, devil's advocate voice
in her head decided to chime in. *Say you do win. What
then? One major problem with singing with Jamie is
he isn't planning on sticking around.*

She wouldn't think about that now. She'd take things
one step at a time. The first one being to prepare the
band for the contest and give them the best chance of
winning.

"It's going to take a lot of work to be ready for
the shelter fund-raiser, but I think we can do it," she
said, trying to regain control of rehearsal. She almost
laughed. Who was she kidding? She hadn't been in control of anything today. "Playing at the Pet Walk will be
a good test run for the state fair."

"You know, the way Jamie sings harmony could add
a new dimension to our sound. We could rework some
of our stuff," Luke added.

And here they were, back on the topic of the day,
Jamie. Had everyone gotten together and plotted to
drive her insane? It was sure starting to feel that way.

"Slow down. We don't know if him playing with us
will work. He might not be able to make the transition
to country music," she said. "If that's the case, he'll just
sing a couple of songs for the shelter benefit. But even
if he does work out, all we've talked about is him helping until we find someone permanent."

Luke smiled. "Who knows. Maybe he'll like playing
with us so much he'll change his religion, so to speak,
and decide to stick around."

THE RANCH WHERE Emma grew up hadn't changed much
in the years since Jamie had last been here. A modest

house that now needed a coat of paint. A massive red barn that looked as if it was straight out of every rural painting he'd ever seen and land guarded by the Rocky Mountains.

Funny, he thought as he parked by the garage and headed inside, how some things changed so much while others stayed the same.

Emma introduced him to the other band members, Grayson and Luke, and the four of them stood and chatted for a couple of minutes. Just small talk. How long they'd been playing together. Their backgrounds. All the basic get-to-know-you stuff.

"Now that the meet and greet is over, let's get to work," Emma said and handed Jamie some music. He glanced through the first few pages. So far so good. Nothing he couldn't handle. Then he hit the third page and twinges of apprehension knotted his gut. A couple measures could trip him up. They weren't so difficult he couldn't have played the music when he was in high school, but now? He wasn't sure. Not with his hand less than 100 percent.

He considered saying they should forget the whole thing, but since Emma had asked him to bring his violin he'd felt almost renewed. Definitely energized from the rush of adrenaline at the thought of a new challenge and playing with a group again. He'd checked out various country bands on the internet and found himself getting excited over the possibilities. He'd even found one band that was appearing in Longmont tonight. Maybe he and Emma could check them out.

As much as he'd thought about the performing possibilities this afternoon, he'd thought about Emma more. He'd wondered what it would be like getting up every morning knowing he'd get to see her. Talk about a work incentive program.

No, he wouldn't give up before he even gave this a shot.

"You ready to give it a try?" she asked.

Talk about a loaded question. He was up for trying a lot of things with Emma. He cleared his throat and tried to get his mind off all the things he'd like to do with her and back on the audition.

He placed the music on the stand she had set up and lifted his violin out of the case. "All set."

Emma counted out two measures. He came in on the fifth. The music flowed out of him, filling him with a passion he hadn't experienced since he'd discovered the sound he could produce with an instrument. Confidence surged in his veins. Emma's voice wrapped around him, drawing him in even further. She reached deep inside him, touching him in a way he never imagined possible. He felt connected. Right in a way he couldn't describe.

When they came to the chorus, the violin part dropped out. He switched to singing harmony to Emma's lead vocals. He could spend all day singing with her. All the uncertainty about his future, the fear and anger at possibly starting over in a new career, disappeared. At the second verse he picked up the violin again. They hit the bridge and he held his own for about ten measures. Then his left ring finger cramped. He botched the fingering and hit one hell of a clunker, throwing off his timing. That left him playing catch up with the band, which never quite happened. Figuring there wasn't any point in jumping back in, he gave up.

A minute later when the song ended there was dead silence. Not that he blamed anyone for not knowing what to say. Hell, he didn't even know what to say since the wooden guy from the auditions had sounded better than he just had. That was bad enough, but his performance made him realize how much work he had ahead of him if he hoped to return to the symphony, but would hard work be enough?

"The vocals were fantastic, but, man, I got to ask you, what happened with the fiddle?" Luke said. "You were good through most of it, but there were some spots that were rough. I've heard you play. Your skills are amazing. What's up?"

Before he could say anything, Emma said, "Not everyone can play country music. Remember when Michael Jordan tried to play baseball? He was an incredible athlete. Arguably the best basketball player ever. Despite that, he couldn't make it in major league baseball. That's how it is with music, too. Maybe country music just isn't Jamie's thing."

Obviously, she hadn't told the guys about his injury, and he realized she was giving him an out, a way to keep his secret if he wanted to. He considered brushing off the question with a vague answer about it being a long story that he'd rather not go into, but decided against it. Keeping people from finding out he'd been let go from the Philharmonic took too much energy and the vacation excuse would only work for so long. When he kept hanging around, people would know something was up. Plus, these guys realized something didn't fit and he wouldn't lie.

As he started explaining about his injury he thought he should have a card printed out to hand to people to save time. Former Classical Musician Sidelined Due to Injury. Physical Issues May or May Not Improve. Please Submit Further Questions in Writing and Wait For the Reply That Will Come When Hell Freezes Over.

"Obviously the injury's affecting my playing. My ring finger is the big issue. It's stiff and doesn't move like it should. If it were my bow hand it wouldn't be any problem." He replaced his violin in the case.

"That sucks," Grayson said.

"You got that right. I came out here to get away."

"Your secret's safe with us. As far as I'm concerned, what's up with your hand isn't anyone else's business," Luke said.

"I appreciate that." The thud as he shut his case sounded like a casket closing and just as final. "Since Avery's started publicizing me singing at the Pet Walk, I'd like to sing with you for that if it's okay with all of you."

"I think you playing fiddle with us could still work."

Jamie stared at Emma, unable to believe what she'd said. *She's either lost her mind or gone tone-deaf.* "You can say that after hearing me play?"

"Understandably you have incredibly high standards, but we could fix the problems you had by tweaking the fiddle parts," she said.

"You mean make them easier?" That hurt. He didn't want a pity job. "No, thanks. I don't need anyone feeling sorry for me."

"If you couldn't cut it on the fiddle I wouldn't make the offer. I don't do pity." Emma stared him straight in the eye, nothing but honesty shining in her gaze. "That ridiculous emotion doesn't do anyone any good. If you discount those couple of measures, you're better than anyone else we've auditioned."

Okay, maybe pity hadn't motivated her offer. He accepted that. A woman with the drive to succeed that Emma possessed wouldn't let anything stand in the way of her goal.

"What you add vocalswise compensates for the little bit we'd have to simplify the fiddle part," Grayson added. "The harmony between you two is amazing. Some of the best stuff I've ever heard."

Luke snapped his fingers. "That gives me an idea. If Jamie sang lead on some numbers it would open up a whole new range of songs for us. We could expand our selections to include more guy-focused stuff and less of this angsty material."

"Yeah, we are a little heavy on the chick songs right now," Grayson agreed.

"Hey, I've written a lot of the material we sing."

"Exactly."

She turned to Jamie. "You've started a mutiny, Fletcher Christian. Thanks."

"Then put a stop to it."

She'd crossed her arms over her chest, her stance stiff and braced. Her brows knit together in thought. He smiled. She was probably weighing the cost of how much jail time she'd get for assaulting Luke and Grayson versus how satisfying it would be to let her anger rip.

Meanwhile, the two knuckleheads rattled on about the songs they could add to the band's repertoire. Jamie cringed. If Grayson and Luke possessed any brains, they'd head for the nearest bomb shelter or, in lieu of that, duck behind the drums for protection from the blast that was heading their way.

"No one is replacing me as the lead singer in this band," Emma said in a low, calm voice, reminding him of the stillness in the eye of a hurricane.

"I'm not saying replace you," Luke backpedaled, uncertainty in his voice. "We'd just change things a little, expand our song choices with Jamie singing the lead every once in a while."

"You saw the comments online. Women love him," Grayson said. "I think Luke's right."

Combined, the two right now didn't have the brains of a scarecrow. Deciding to step in before Emma set them on fire with her death-ray stare, Jamie said, "I don't want any part of singing lead." He refused to hurt Emma like that. When Luke looked as if he might continue pleading his case, Jamie continued, "That's non-negotiable."

His stern no-nonsense tone left everyone clear that the discussion had ended. Out of his peripheral vision he caught Emma's reaction of utter shock. Why did she find what he'd said so hard to believe? Had she really thought he'd come in to her band, take over and shove her aside?

I don't date musicians. They're self-centered and about as reliable as a fortune-teller.

Damn. She'd dated some real winners. Starting with the guy who'd got her pregnant and bailed on her.

Recovering from her shock, she smiled at him, her eyes filled with gratitude. "Now that we've settled that, can we get back to preparing for the concert next weekend?"

"Are you sure you're all okay with changing the violin parts?" he asked, still not sure. Then he almost smiled. What was he thinking? If she wasn't happy with something everyone within three counties would know the fact.

"I thought we'd dealt with that issue, too. We're all okay with it." She glanced pointedly at Luke and Grayson, who nodded. "I'm not making the offer out of pity.

I truly believe it's the best decision for the band. Now, are you in or not?"

"I'm in. I can at least help you out until you find someone permanent."

"If you could agree to stay until the state fair competition that would be great. Our chances of finding someone before that don't look good."

"Deal."

For the next couple of hours they ran through the band's numbers with him marking the measures that gave him trouble. The vocals, the part he would've thought needed work, felt natural and were almost effortless.

When they quit for the day and Luke and Grayson had gone home, Jamie turned to Emma. "I was planning on checking out a band playing at Dick's Tavern in Longmont tonight. How about we get some dinner, talk about those songs that need modification and then listen to the band?"

Before he even finished, she was shaking her head. "That's not a good idea. One of the rules we have is that band members don't socialize. We've found that tends to—" She paused and chewed on her lip.

Jamie braced himself. This ought to be good. When she thought that hard, he'd discovered she was trying to decide between brutal honesty or if she should soften the blow.

"Let's just say having personal relationships complicates things."

"Is this about last night? It was just a kiss."

He wanted to laugh at his ridiculous comment and how he'd managed to deliver the statement with a straight face. Just a kiss? Hardly.

"It doesn't matter because I have plans tonight."

"I grew up with two sisters. I'm fluent in female speak. When a woman uses the vague 'I have plans tonight' comment instead of saying what her plans are, it usually means one of two things. Either she isn't attracted to the guy, but doesn't want to hurt his feelings, or she is attracted to him, but she's afraid of what she feels."

"Then here's the truth. I'm not interested, but I didn't want to hurt your feelings."

This time he did laugh. The little minx thought he wouldn't see through her lie? Wrong. "No way are you selling me that three-legged horse."

She raised her eyebrow at his word choice.

Really? He couldn't use a Western expression? He'd spent enough time in Estes Park over the years that he'd outgrown greenhorn status. Ignoring her expression, he continued. "I know that's not true. There was enough heat between us to make the devil sweat, and it wasn't just on my part, or did I imagine you crawling onto my lap last night?"

"Talk about arrogance."

But he noticed she didn't deny what he'd said. "It's not arrogant if it's the truth." He stepped closer, his gaze zeroing in on her as the memories of kissing her revved his body up all over again. He smiled. She stepped back. Yup, he'd pegged it right. She felt something, but it scared her.

"I'm not going to dignify your comment by responding because there's no way I'm going to change your mind. Wrong though you may be."

"What I want to know," he said as he closed the distance between them again, "is why what you feel for me scares you."

Her eyes darkened and she tilted her chin up at him.

He had to bite his lip to keep from smiling as she rose to the bait he'd put in front of her. "That'll be the day, and I'll prove how wrong you are. Seeing a band tonight is a great idea. Not only can we work on the music, we can talk about the band's performance, the pros and cons. It'll help you get ready for our first performance."

"Should I drive or do you want to?"

"I think separate cars. That way we're both free to leave whenever we need to."

He thought about pressing the issue, but a smart man knew when to walk away from the table before he lost everything he'd won. "Fine. Meet you at Dick's Tavern."

Chapter Ten

When Emma and Jamie walked into Dick's Tavern, she vowed to prove she wasn't *that* attracted to him—no way could she make either one of them believe there wasn't *any* attraction. She wouldn't touch the rest of what he'd said, that she was scared of what she felt for him, with gloves, a ten-foot pole and a shark cage. Mainly because there was no disproving the truth.

Dick's, while still possessing a down-home feel, was more upscale than Halligan's. There were simple white tablecloths on the tables and less neon over the bar and stage.

Being with Jamie tonight and working together would be a good thing. She'd spend time with him and realize what she felt with him when they sang couldn't survive off the stage. With that gone there'd be nothing of substance left and her vision would be clear.

But what if she didn't find that? So what if she was attracted to him? It was probably nothing more than her body's hormonal cravings from her dating drought. She could keep things between them professional and she could maintain control.

She'd see he was no different than every other musician she'd known. They all craved the spotlight, and if she let him, slowly he'd start taking more of hers.

If that's what he wanted then why had he turned down Luke's suggestion that he sing lead on a few songs?

"I noticed you making notes on the music during rehearsal," Emma said once she and Jamie were seated.

"A few places gave me trouble, but I think I can change the rhythm a little or the notes without changing the integrity of what you wrote."

She nodded and opened her menu. Okay, what should she do now? And she thought first dates were awkward. When was the last time she'd had a first date? That would've been with Clint. What? Almost three years ago?

This wasn't a date, she told herself. A business meeting with food, followed by studying a band. That's what this was.

Simple.

Right. Just like milking a bull.

"I'll work on making the changes tomorrow," Jamie said.

"We'll have to put in a lot of rehearsal time before the state fair, but if you work on the music on your own, I think we can be ready."

"Just let me know the rehearsal times. I'll clear things with Mick."

Awkward silence stretched until the perky waitress dressed in jeans and a two-sizes-too-small Dick's Tavern T-shirt popped up at their table to take their orders. Emma couldn't miss the woman giving Jamie the once-over.

"This band's pretty good," Emma said once they'd placed their order and Miss Perky had bounced off. "Though they don't have a fiddle player, you can still learn a lot from them. Watch for how they move on the stage and how they connect with the audience."

Yeah. Because Jamie needs so much help in those two areas.

"Do you ever think about anything but work?"

"The country music business is very competitive. I need to stay focused." Emma reached for her water glass to give her something to do.

"There's focused, and there's not having a life outside work."

Emma cringed. There was that phrase again. What was it with everyone lately? "Tell me you weren't just as driven when you were with the Philharmonic."

"You got me there. I was, but hurting my hand's given me a new perspective."

When he flexed his hand she regretted bringing up the subject. What would she do if she couldn't play the guitar or sing anymore? What else would she have in her life? Not a whole lot, but wasn't that what she wanted? Sacrifices had to be made for her career, to move forward to the next level.

Wanting to lighten up the conversation, she said, "Growing up with a house full of brothers was noisy, wild and messy. I wanted to hang around with them, but they were always trying to ditch me. What was it like growing up with only sisters?"

"The worst thing was the bathroom. Not only did I have to schedule time to use it, but by the time I got in, the hot water was usually gone."

"That's rough."

"Tell me about it. We lived in Pennsylvania. Do you know how awful a cold shower is in the winter?"

"I bet it gets the blood flowing."

"When it doesn't give a guy a heart attack."

"Come on. Quit whining. It made you tough," Emma said with a grin.

The waitress brought their food, eyed Jamie and asked if there was anything else he needed. Not them, but just him. As though Emma was chopped liver or invisible. Maybe she was invisible chopped liver. Anyway, when Jamie said no, they were good, without even glancing at the woman, the obviously disappointed server flitted off.

Interesting.

"Finally I decided I'd sacrifice sleep for hot water, and set my alarm for oh-dark-thirty to get up before my sisters. What about you? What was the worst part of being the only girl?"

"They used to climb trees to get away from me."

"How long did it take you to learn to climb one, too?"

"How come you're so sure that's what I did? Maybe I gave up and quit trying to keep up with them."

"You? No way. You'd see that as admitting defeat. You're driven and when you set your mind to something there's no stopping you."

The fact that he had her so well pegged both irritated and pleased her. "It took me every day after school for a whole week, and cost me more scraped knees and arms than I could count, but I did it."

AFTER DINNER THEY moved to a smaller table closer to the stage. When the band started playing, Emma relaxed now that she had a comfortable subject to focus on. "See how the lead singer connects visually with the audience? He nods at people and smiles when there's a break in the vocals. He's also good about moving around on the stage."

"The guy's all over the place."

"He doesn't want either side of the audience to feel slighted."

"Since I'm not the lead singer, I won't have to worry about that."

"Oh, yes, you will. I don't want all the women trampling each other because they want to get a better vantage point to ogle you," she teased. "What we need to do is occasionally have you and Luke switch sides. That way no one will feel slighted."

"You really think about stuff like this?"

"Details matter. Those subtleties can make the difference between getting stuck playing local clubs and breaking out. Have you thought about what you're going to wear for the concert?"

"You're kidding, right?"

She shook her head. "There are more options than you'd think. One is the T-shirt and jeans, cowboy style. There's the more plaid Western shirt and jeans look. There's also—"

"You are not going to give me a how-to-dress class. Let's dance."

The word *yes* almost popped out of her mouth. Almost. She loved dancing, and Jamie would be a great partner. The man could move.

How long had it been since she'd gone dancing? Most weekend nights she performed with the band. On weeknights she had her day job to think about. What would it be like to let go of being cautious, of not thinking everything through ten times before acting? Of just living a little?

Too tempting. Too wonderful. Too scary to consider. Business meeting with food and a band. Remember?

"We can't see what the band's doing if we're on the dance floor."

"Come on. For the past twenty minutes you've been analyzing the band's every move and teaching a class. Time for recess."

"I'm trying to prepare you for the concert."

"Don't get me wrong. I appreciate the effort, but I need a break so everything you've said can soak in. Otherwise information is going to leak out my ears."

His comment made her smile. She had given him a lot to process. She glanced at the people on the dance floor doing the "Cotton-Eyed Joe." "You can line dance?"

"I took a class. A friend said it would be a good way for us to meet women."

"That sounds like something my brothers would say."

"Hey, there's always got to be a payoff for the hard work." He pushed his chair back from the table. "You need to lighten up a little and have some fun."

Fun? What is this fun of which you speak? "I have fun. You saw me at Halligan's with Avery and Stacy." She wouldn't mention that before that Friday night it had been more than two months since she'd gone out with friends.

"Fine. I concede. You don't need to have any fun, but take pity on me, because I sure do." When she hesitated, he continued, "Don't turn me into the lonely guy at the bar who has to ask a stranger to dance."

He really thought that line would work? She'd seen most of the women in the place eyeing him since they'd walked in, as they tried to decipher her and Jamie's relationship. Were they out on a date? Friends? Coworkers?

Join the club, girls. I'm still trying to figure that out, too.

"You wouldn't ask someone else to dance and leave me sitting here. That's not your style," she countered.

"Wanna bet?"

Her gaze locked with his as she tried to decide whether or not to call his bluff. Avery's voice popped into Emma's head. *Are you so sure your life doesn't need shaking up?*

Shaking it up would be one thing. Putting it into a blender and turning the machine on frappé was something else. She had a feeling getting involved with Jamie would be the latter.

But what could a couple of dances hurt? Especially line dancing. No touching involved there. "Let's see if you can keep up with me, city boy."

For most of the next set, Jamie didn't keep up with her. He about left her in his dust. Through the "Watermelon Crawl," the "Copperhead Road" and "The Slide." And she'd talked to him about how he should move onstage. She felt more than a bit stupid over having done that.

"Not bad," she said when the band switched to playing a slow song.

"For a city boy?"

"For anybody. You've got some moves."

He leaned toward her. "You have no idea."

Boy, she'd stepped right into that one. The question was how did she get out of this mess?

His gaze locked on hers, hot, steamy and inviting as he moved toward her. When he stood inches in front of her, he slipped his arm around her waist.

A little voice in her head told her to run, not walk, to the nearest exit.

Despite knowing it wasn't the best idea, she stepped into his arms.

JAMIE SMILED, AND THOUGHT this was what he'd been waiting for all night—to hold Emma.

Funny thing. The more they'd rehearsed tonight, and the more they connected onstage, the more distant she became when the music stopped. He swore he saw her withdrawing into herself, while he felt the opposite. The time he spent with her left him wanting, and not just physically.

Nothing in his life had ever felt as right as being with Emma. He could be himself. He found a serenity with her that he'd never found with anyone else.

She leaned to the right to see around him. "You should check out the band. They have a completely different presence when they play a slow song like this one."

"Why are you pushing me away?"

Her gaze jerked back to his. When she opened her mouth, he held up a hand. "Don't bother to deny it because I won't believe you."

"You don't beat around an issue, do you?"

"What point is there? All avoiding something does is create confusion, hurt feelings, and it makes us miss out on some great experiences."

"What makes you think I'm pushing you away?"

"Except when we're singing, you're distant at rehearsal. And when we start talking about anything but work, you get nervous."

"It's not you, it's me."

He laughed. "I can't believe you said that. It's got to be the oldest cop-out line in the book. You think too much. This is pretty simple. I enjoy your company, and I thought you enjoyed mine."

"I do." Her voice sounded almost pained. As if she were on the witness stand and the prosecuting attorney had gotten her to admit she'd seen her best friend rob a store clerk at gunpoint.

"Don't sound so thrilled. Is liking me, wanting to spend time with me, such a bad thing?"

"I have to stay focused. I'm so close. I could finally have the success I've waited and worked so long for."

"You know what they say. All work and no play makes—"

"Emma a boring girl?" she finished for him, her gaze hooded.

His hand slid to the spot where her neck and shoulder met. His thumb gently caressed the sensitive area. He felt a shudder ripple through her. "I was going to say 'makes Emma come up empty for new song material.'"

"Right. That's what you were going to say."

"You have a gift, but when we were practicing I realized something. I can tell the newer pieces you've written the minute I start playing. There's not as much of you in those songs."

He resisted the urge to pull her closer. The vein in her neck throbbed at a frantic pace, contradicting the cool image she tried so hard to present to the world, but she couldn't fool him. He knew to back off, though, and handle her with a light touch. The best things were worth the wait.

"I don't know what you mean."

"You're holding back. From me. From life." He leaned closer until he felt her warm breath against his cheek. "We enjoy each other's company. We have fun. No big deal. Is that so bad?"

He saw her shut down. Her gaze grew distant. She stepped out of his arms and crossed her arms over her chest as if drawing herself inward.

So much for his light touch.

"I think it's time I went home."

He nodded and followed her out of the restaurant. When they reached her car, he said, "I'll follow you to make sure you don't have any problems."

"You know what? Before you got here, I managed to get everywhere safe and sound all on my own."

"It has nothing to do with you not being capable. There are a lot of weird people in the world. Don't you listen to the news? It's not smart for a woman to be out alone this time of night."

"This isn't New York City."

"Why does my common courtesy bother you so much?"

"Fine. Follow me home." She yanked open her car door, slid inside and slammed it shut with enough force to rattle the windows across the street.

He smiled as he got in his car and followed Emma back to Estes Park. She wasted so much energy trying to prove how tough she was. That she didn't need anyone. That she didn't need even small courtesies from him. Was it just him, or did she act that way with everyone?

When they reached her apartment building, he joined her on the walkway. "You followed me home. I'm fine. I made it here in one piece. You've done your gentlemanly duty. You can leave."

The more she pushed him away, the more he wanted to reach the woman behind the wall. The one he'd seen glimpses of and felt so drawn to.

"I had fun tonight."

"I'm not going to ask you to come into my apartment."

"I didn't expect you to." She tilted her head and eyed him as if trying to decide whether he meant what he'd just said. "Remember, I don't beat around the bush. When I say something, I mean it."

He leaned forward and brushed his lips against hers in a light kiss. Then, without another word, he walked back to his car. Yup. Slow and steady. That's what would win the race with Emma.

AFTER THE NIGHT at Dick's Tavern, Emma changed her game plan. Denying her emotions hadn't worked. Instead she admitted the fact she was attracted to Jamie and that her body came alive anytime he was around. There. The first step to dealing with a problem was openly acknowledging what the problem was.

Now that she'd done that, she developed a two-part solution. Quit fighting her feelings and instead channel all the sexual energy she felt for him into her music. But the key to success lay in the second part of her plan. Avoid Jamie any other time other than rehearsals.

And that's what she did. She avoided Halligan's during the day since Mick had scheduled Jamie to work then to accommodate their rehearsal schedule. She'd started closing her door when she worked in her office in case he showed up. Yesterday when he'd brought Trooper in for a weigh-in she'd pretended she wasn't there when he'd knocked on her door. While she couldn't say she was happier, she at least felt more under control.

Today when Jamie walked into the garage for rehearsal he marched straight over to her, stopping a few inches in front of her, his dark gaze intent and determined. "How long are you going to avoid me and give me the cold-shoulder treatment during rehearsals?"

"I don't know what you're talking about. With the Pet Walk this weekend it's been crazy at the shelter. I have so many last-minute things to see to, it hasn't left me much time for anything else."

"At least be honest with me. I deserve that."

Direct hit. "All right. I have been avoiding you. My life has been a disaster the past two years. I finally have it back on track. I don't want anything to mess this up."

"And you think I'd do that?"

"I need to stay focused."

He stepped closer. He stood so close she could see the tiny golden flecks in his brown eyes, but she refused to retreat. "Are you saying you can't handle me?"

Her throat grew dry. Then she realized what he was doing. She'd missed the first time he'd manipulated her by saying she couldn't handle something to get her to go to Dick's Tavern, but his ploy wasn't going to work this time.

"I know what you're doing. I don't know how I missed the old challenge ploy after all the times my brothers pulled that scam on me growing up, but I'm on to you now."

He had the nerve to smile.

She stood there, trying to think of the best comeback to wipe that grin off his face, but before she could, the garage door squeaked open. Luke sauntered in, followed by Grayson.

"Everyone's talking about us playing at the Pet Walk." Luke froze and glanced between her and Jamie. "Everything cool between you two? You look like we interrupted something."

"We're fine," Emma said. "I'm so glad everyone's talking about the concert. From what Avery said, ticket sales are up, so we should have an even better turnout than last year. Now we need to get to work and run through the numbers we plan to do this weekend."

Once they started rehearsing, her tension eased. This she could handle. Her world righted as they worked on the music for the concert.

"I thought we'd have to change that section, but you breezed right through it," Emma said when they finished the latest number.

"That surprised me, too." Jamie's face filled with pride.

"You're sounding more like the guy who played with the Philharmonic every day."

At Luke's comment a thought bolted through Emma. Jamie's hand *had* improved. As their rehearsals had progressed, she'd realized that fact, but she hadn't thought about the implications. Somewhere along the line, she'd forgotten about looking for a permanent replacement. What if they did win the contest, and Jamie decided he wanted to return to classical music? What if a position opened up with the Philharmonic? What if he decided to find another symphony? The thought of him leaving, of not seeing him again, left her shaken.

Hadn't Avery told her to quit borrowing trouble? Now seemed like a good time to put that into practice. If they won, or rather, when they won the contest, she corrected, and if Jamie decided to leave, they'd find someone else. He wasn't the only fiddle player in the country. With Phillip Brandise's interest, she bet some of the musicians who claimed they were happy with their bands wouldn't be quite so content if she contacted them again. The tightness in her chest loosened. A little. Not as much as it should have, though.

"I don't know about the rest of you, but I'm done for the night," Luke said.

"I'd like to run through a few more numbers. With

the Pet Walk this weekend and the competition soon after that, I could use the extra practice," Jamie said.

"Trust me, you're ready." The doubt in his eyes surprised Emma, as did her twinge of concern. "Are there any numbers in particular you're nervous about?"

Before he could answer, Emma's phone rang. She mumbled an apology and explained with the Pet Walk she needed to take the call.

"Emma Donovan?" the shaky male voice on the other end asked.

"That's me. What can I do for you?" she said, expecting to hear a question about the Pet Walk or the concert.

"This is Mark Sinclair. The agency gave me your phone number. My wife and I adopted your son. We named him Andrew."

She whispered the name, testing it out. Her son's name was Andrew.

When she'd talked to the agency about being open to communication with the adoptive parents, she wasn't sure she expected this day would ever come. Or if she did, she imagined it way in the future. Now faced with the reality, questions tumbled over each other in her head, creating an indiscernible chaos.

"I've been thinking about your family a lot lately. How is Andrew?"

"That's why I'm calling," Mark's voice broke. "He's sick. Very sick, and we need your help."

Panic, white-hot and blinding, rushed through her. She braced against the pain, forcing it back. Now all the odd feelings she'd been having about her son and why he'd been in her thoughts so much made sense. Somehow she'd known he needed her. "What's wrong and what can I do to help?"

"Andrew had a cancerous brain tumor. The doctor

believes they got it all in the surgery, but the chemo-
therapy damaged his bone marrow. Now he needs a
transplant. Carmen and I were tested, but we're not a
match. Andrew's doctor says one of his birth parents
is his best chance."

She should have been careful what she wished for.
She'd wanted to know about her son, possibly even become a part of his life, but not like this. Not because
he was sick. What she wouldn't give to be able to trade
places with him.

"Of course I'll get tested. Can a doctor's office take
care of it or do I need to go to the hospital?"

"Any doctor can take the sample. All he needs to
do is swab the inside of your cheek and send it off for
typing." Mark said he'd text her the details on the typing she needed to request and where the results should
be sent.

She nodded and glanced at her watch. Her vision
blurred and she swiped a hand over her eyes, surprised
when they came away wet. Four o'clock. Would her doctor's office still be open this late on Saturday afternoon?
If not, maybe she could go to one of those doc-in-a-
box-type places. "I'll get the test taken care of today."

"I appreciate you doing this," Mark said, and then he
sighed. "I'm praying you'll be a match, but in case you
aren't, do you know how I can reach the birth father?
The agency doesn't have current information on him."

That didn't surprise her. When she'd asked Tucker if
he'd wanted to meet with prospective parents, he'd said
whoever she chose was fine with him. Then he'd told
her to send him whatever he needed to sign in order to
relinquish his parental right and said he never wanted
to discuss the "issue" again. How could any man refer
to his child like that?

He certainly wouldn't be thrilled with anyone contacting him. Too bad. No matter how hard she and Tucker wished otherwise, they were connected and always would be. How could one small moment in time change her life so profoundly and on so many levels? She hadn't realized that when she'd become intimate with Tucker. All she'd thought about was how much she loved him. "I haven't talked to him since we broke up, but his parents still live here part-time."

Thankfully once his career had taken off, Tucker had quit visiting his parents in Estes Park, instead preferring to fly them to Nashville. Then, a couple of years ago, he'd bought a house for them there, as well.

"We'd like him to get tested, too. In case you're not a match."

"I'll text you their phone number, but hopefully we won't have to worry about that. I'm praying I'll be a match." But she couldn't blame Andrew's father for wanting to hedge his bets.

After she ended the call, what she'd learned tumbled over in her mind. Brain tumor. Cancer. Chemo. Her heart bled for the child she'd never known. No seven-year-old should have to deal with those issues. A coldness swept through her.

"What's wrong?"

The concern in Jamie's voice and his warm hand on her icy skin broke through the wall holding her together. Tears stung her eyes and her chest tightened. Her heart banged against her ribs, threatening to break through. "Something's come up. We're done for the day." Then, not wanting anyone to see her fall apart even further, she darted out of the garage.

She ran for the safety of her car. Her brain wouldn't function. All she could think about was the fact that the son she'd never had a chance to know might die. Tears spilled down her cheeks. Her shoulders shook from the pain coursing through her.

The passenger door opened, startling her. She swiped a hand over her face, wiping away the remnants of her tears as Jamie slid into the passenger seat. "Want to tell me what's wrong?"

She tried to speak but she couldn't push the words past her tight throat.

"Take deep breaths." His reassuring voice broke through her fog. Her gaze sought his calm one as she shut out everything but him and matched her breathing with his. "You mentioned a test. Start with that."

"My son's name is Andrew and he's sick. That was his father, Mark, on the phone. He needs a bone marrow transplant. I need to get tested to see if I'm a match."

"What do you need to do? Can a doctor do the test?"

She nodded. "But I don't remember if my family practitioner is open late on Saturdays."

"Call and find out."

She nodded. Her hands shook as she opened her purse and dug around for her phone. After she called the office, she turned to Jamie. "They're open until five. The nurse said they'll work me in when I get there." The fear welled up inside of her again. "Andrew's father said he had a brain tumor. The chemo has damaged his bone marrow so that's why he needs the transplant."

Saying the words out loud made them so much more real. She bit her lip to keep from crying. What if she wasn't a match? Dizziness swamped her.

"Change places with me."

She turned to Jamie. "What? I don't understand."

"You're in no shape to drive. You're pale and you're shaking."

She glanced at her hands. Yup. Shaking like a newborn foal. "I guess the fact that I didn't eat lunch, combined with the stress, is getting to me. I'll be fine. I just need a minute to calm down."

"There's no way in hell I'm letting you drive."

She started to argue but stopped. He had the same stubborn look in his eyes as he'd had that night they'd found Trooper and he hadn't wanted her going out alone. "You're going to be stubborn about this again, aren't you?"

"You got that right."

Okay, then. That settled that. She opened her car door. As she changed places with him, she had to admit she kind of liked him going all caveman and laying down the law because he was concerned about her.

Chapter Eleven

As Jamie sat waiting for Emma, he couldn't help but admire her strength. When she'd first told him about the phone call in the car he'd seen how pale she was. The pain had been evident in her face and in her voice. Then, right before his eyes, she'd sucked it up, turned all-business and went into get-the-job-done mode. She'd never considered any option but helping her son.

The woman's backbone was made of steel, but her heart was as sweet, soft and gooey as one of his mom's homemade chocolate chip cookies.

What would it be like to have a woman like that in his life? One he could count on when things got tough. Oh, let's say when a guy hurt his hand and had to face the fact that he might need to start over in a new career?

A woman like Emma would give him the strength to tackle the worst life could throw at him, and she wouldn't stand behind him. She'd stand beside him every step of the way.

He thought about rehearsal. Since he'd been playing with the band he'd noticed the dexterity returning to his left hand, but today showed him how far he'd come. Last week he wouldn't have been able to play the song he had today.

Maybe it was time to try playing music he'd performed with the Philharmonic. That would be the true test. He should do that tonight when he got back to Mick's.

He flexed his hand. Funny how it didn't look any different, and yet he knew it was. Maybe he wouldn't be forced to reinvent himself after all. The thought should have him ready to crack open the champagne, but instead he found the idea unsettling. If he returned to his old life, what would he find waiting for him other than his career? Not much more than a few acquaintances who, once he was out of sight, had forgotten he existed.

And what about Emma?

What had he said to her at Dick's Tavern that night? Something like they enjoyed each other's company and had fun. No big deal. He'd been so full of it.

She understood him in a way no one else did. Her enthusiasm, her love of music was infectious. He found himself looking forward to seeing her every day.

The door to the exam rooms opened and she walked out, her face drawn. "All done. They've put a rush on the test because Andrew is so sick." Her voice broke and tears pooled in her eyes. He closed the distance between them and wrapped his arms around her. "Dr. Sampson said I should know in a few days."

"You're doing all you can."

"But what if it's not enough? What if I'm not a match?"

"We'll deal with that if it happens."

His words stunned him. We? When had he and Emma become a we? The thought left him weak.

Needing to lighten the mood for her sake as well as his, he said, "I've been thinking about what to wear to the concert."

She tilted her head and eyed him. "This from the guy

who gave me a hard time when I brought up the subject at Dick's Tavern?"

"Yup. I hadn't thought about it then, but now I have. I've got a black T-shirt, but I don't have a cowboy hat or boots." What if the people who purchased tickets pegged him as a smug city boy trying to be something he wasn't?

"Go to Rocky Mountain Outfitters. That's where my brothers shop. That is, when they hit the point where they've either got to wash clothes or buy new ones."

"I could use your opinion," he said as they walked through the office building toward the parking lot.

"Whatever you pick out will be fine."

Was she purposely making this tough? Weren't women supposed to be good at picking up on hints? He shoved his hands in his front pockets and fingered the coins there. "I'm nervous about the concert."

"You've been onstage before. It's no different than the night we sang at Mick's place."

"Oh, yes, it is. People are paying to hear me this time. I don't want to disappoint anyone."

"What do your clothes have to do with that?"

"You really are slow on the uptake today."

"You'd better be nice. It sounds like you're trying to work up to asking me for a favor, and those who don't ask nicely get bubkes."

Now he understood. This was payback for him playing dumb when she'd hinted at him joining the band. "I'm classically trained. Everyone was great at Halligan's when I sang, but that was my grandfather's bar. A paying audience might not be as forgiving. I live in New York City. I'm a city boy, as you're so fond of reminding me. I don't want to look like I'm playing dress-up."

"Come on, then. We'll go shopping."

EMMA KNEW JAMIE wanted her help the minute he mentioned he was thinking about what he should wear for the concert, but couldn't resist giving him a hard time. Then he'd gone and ruined her fun by telling her the truth and sharing another confidence. Damn him.

I'm nervous about the concert. I don't want to look like I'm playing dress-up.

His honesty reached inside her, drawing her in like nothing else could. She thought about what he'd shared with her in the barn, how he sometimes felt on the outside looking in with his family. That's what this was about. He wanted to belong.

The man really should take a good long look in the mirror sometime. With his voice and looks, women wouldn't notice, much less care, what he wore onstage. But she hadn't told him that, so instead here she was shopping with him.

Once they stood inside Rocky Mountain Outfitters, Jamie picked up a leather belt with rhinestones, silver studs and a huge shiny buckle. "When we were at Dick's, you said there were different country singer styles. You never mentioned country bling. The lights bouncing off this would be great. It would make me stand out onstage. Maybe this is the look I should go for."

"I knew you were one of those guys who needed the spotlight to be on him. This only proves it," she teased. But didn't people use joking as a nonthreatening way of telling the truth? "The next thing we know, you'll be asking for a spot dedicated just for you."

"If that's what I wanted, I'd have asked you about this." He shook his head and picked up a belt with an even gaudier buckle. "But since you brought up the lighting issue—"

"I dare you to wear that. To even try it on."

"You sure you want to do that?" His stubborn I'm-not-backing-down gaze drilled through her.

Who knew that he could produce the look on demand when he clearly wasn't annoyed, and only teasing her? She shuddered with exaggerated horror. "Oops. I forgot how stubborn you can be. I take back the dare."

"That's right. You better, woman."

"Can I help either of you find anything or maybe referee?" Emma recognized the voice, and froze.

She'd hoped Harper wouldn't be in. Leave it to the older woman to pop up and spoil all the fun.

Harper, dressed in jeans and the same brown-and-turquoise paisley Western shirt as displayed in the front window, shook her head. "I never knew what my grandmother meant when she said one couple's fighting is another one's dancing until now. You two are having way too much fun trying to get under each other's skin."

"Jamie, this is Harper Stinson, Rocky Mountain Outfitter's owner and board president of the Estes Park animal shelter."

"Pleased to meet you, ma'am. I'm here to find something to wear for the shelter concert. Emma told me she'd help, but all she's doing so far is giving me a hard time."

"Don't blame me when you haven't been taking this seriously. I'm not the one who'll be performing in athletic shoes."

"Don't start any more of that dancing, you two," Harper said. "The boots are this way. I'll help you out because no way am I letting you go onstage for the shelter fund-raiser in tennis shoes, and we'll do something about a shirt while we're at it." She nodded toward Emma. "Between the two of us, we'll take care of things."

AFTER THE NIGHT spent shopping with Jamie, Emma decided she was done fighting what she felt for him. She was tired of being strong, focused and directed all the time. More important, she was tired of being alone.

Not that she thought she'd found her soul mate or anything crazy like that. She believed the soul mate thing was as real as Bigfoot—but Jamie made her laugh, something she hadn't done enough of since her mother had gotten sick, and for right now, that was enough. No harm. No foul. That became her motto.

From that night on, she and Jamie went out to eat after rehearsals and talked about whatever came to mind. Music, their childhoods. She learned he'd secretly listened to country music in high school. Sometimes they worked on music and had even started writing some songs together. A couple of times they went hiking or horseback riding. Nothing special, and yet their time together fed her soul.

Now today Emma stood in the parking lot at Stanley Park unloading tables and chairs from the shelter van for the Pet Walk when Jamie pulled up. He'd been such a rock for her when she'd found out about Andrew. It would have been so easy to fall apart, and she probably would have if it hadn't been for Jamie.

He got out of Mick's battered Chevy truck, looking way too good for this early in the morning, wearing one of the shirts he'd bought when they'd gone shopping. As it happened, her favorite, the tan-and-brown plaid that matched his coffee-colored eyes.

Before, when he was dressed in khakis and a polo

shirt, he'd looked... She searched for the right word. *Restrained. Reserved.* Almost as if he was apart from everyone and everything around him. Now a relaxed air surrounded him. He appeared at ease. Almost as if she was seeing the inner man for the first time. He looked as though he'd been here his entire life. As though he belonged.

She nodded toward his feet. "Good-looking boots."

"Do I pass muster?"

"You'll do."

Anytime. Anywhere.

The image of him kissing her in Mick's living room flashed in her mind, sending her already racing pulse even higher. What would've happened if she hadn't left? Clothes would have gone flying and they'd have been all over each other, more than likely. Last week the idea had left her shaking in her boots, but this week the idea sounded a whole lot better.

What was she thinking? She needed to snap out of it. Abstinence was rotting her brain. That was the problem.

"It's too bad I'm working today. I bet Trooper would love being out here," Jamie said.

She grinned. "I've seen that look before. Has he found a forever home?"

"I don't know if Mick will want to adopt him or not."

"That wasn't who I was talking about. What about you?"

"My apartment doesn't allow pets."

The boulder came out of nowhere and rolled right over her. How could she have forgotten the fact that Jamie being here was only temporary? Luke's words flashed in her mind. *Maybe he'll like playing with us so much he'll change his religion, so to speak, and decide to stick around.*

See what happens when you have expectations? When you start hoping?

She reached for a stack of chairs, but he brushed her hand aside. "You need all these unloaded?"

"You offering to help?" When he nodded, she pointed toward the tent that had been set up at the park entrance. If nothing else, she'd be grateful for the free labor today, which meant fewer aching muscles tomorrow for her. "They go at the registration desk."

"I'm all yours until nine."

If only that were true.

Where had that thought come from and how could she get rid of it? Lighten things up and focus on work. That would do the trick. "All right, assistant. Let's get these tables and chairs set up."

"YOU AND EMMA have been spending a lot of time together," Mick said a couple of hours later when Jamie arrived at the pavilion to help set up the food booth.

"That's about as smooth a move into a conversation as a gravel road." Since she'd found out about her son, their relationship had changed, but the hell if he knew what it had changed into. While most nights they grabbed a bite to eat after rehearsals, he couldn't really say they were dating, and yet, they were more than friends because whenever they were together the air crackled with sexual tension. "With getting ready for today and the state fair coming up, we've been rehearsing a lot."

Mick grinned like a matchmaking momma. "You sure that's all it's been? Rehearsing? The rumor mill says you two have been out almost every night. That sounds like dating to me."

"You're getting as bad as an old woman."

Jamie reached into a box and started unpacking serving utensils and packets of plastic silverware. He thought about what Emma had told him about her baby's father. *He made it clear he wanted nothing to do with fatherhood.* His curiosity ate at him, but he hadn't asked Emma for fear of opening up old wounds. "Since you brought up the dating subject, Emma says she doesn't get involved with musicians. Is that because of her baby's father?"

"That Tucker Mathis always was an ass and never was good enough for Emma."

"Tucker Mathis? As in, part of one of the hottest acts in country music right now?" That's who'd fathered Emma's child?

Mick nodded. "Gene told me he was messin' around on Emma when they were living together in Nashville. She was working two jobs to support them while he was working on making 'industry connections.' Well, he made 'em, all right, with anything in a skirt. Then, when Emma told him she was pregnant, he left her and moved in with that blonde-in-a-bottle he sings with now."

So many things made sense now. Tucker had gone on to live the dream while Emma had gone home to a family embarrassed by her pregnancy and had struggled with the decision of whether or not to give her child up for adoption.

Jamie's thoughts turned to what Emma had said about her last band. *Turned out they'd already replaced me. They just forgot to tell me.*

He'd bet she'd been dating someone in that band when she'd come back to Estes Park to take care of her mother. There had been too much pain in her eyes when she'd told him about that. The betrayal had been deeper. More personal.

"Gene also said the song that got Tucker his first record deal was one he and Emma wrote together. Though, of course, he claims different."

"Why didn't she take him to court?" What a stupid question. Cases like that cost money, were emotionally exhausting and lengthy. After what she'd gone through, how could Emma have dealt with taking Tucker to court? "Never mind. I know the reasons."

No wonder she'd sworn off musicians.

"Hey, Mick, you open for business?" a fortysomething man with a German shepherd on a leash called out from across the walkway.

"Sure are. Come on over, Sam," Mick replied.

"Good, because I'm so hungry those dog biscuits at the Puppy Palace booth are starting to look good. Give me one of your brats instead." Sam dug out his wallet, found a five and handed the bill to Jamie. "It's good to see you here helping Mick. A man his age should have family around."

"I'm glad to do it."

"I got my ticket for the concert," Henry said as he joined the growing line. "When the band makes it big, I expect you and Emma to give me credit since your changing careers and joining Maroon Peak Pass was my idea." The older man scratched his chin. "In fact, I think coming up with the suggestion entitles me to free CDs for life. Don't you?"

Changing careers. Jamie froze. When had he done that? He hadn't as far as he knew. Had he latched on to Emma's dream to fill the void in his life and to avoid having to face deciding about his future?

"I think you're putting the cart in front of the horse there, Henry. All I'm doing is helping the band out. We're just testing the waters." Isn't that what he and

Emma had said? "It may not work out. People may not accept a classically trained violinist playing country music."

Or it could be everyone would think he stunk. Could be he'd choke or hate playing more popular music. Great time to remember that he could fall flat on his face. That'll give him confidence to walk onto the stage.

"I love that Darius Rucker. Then I come to learn he was in some Top 40 band years ago," the middle aged woman waiting behind Henry said. "It was some band with a funny fish name. Anyway, country music fans have accepted him. If they can do that, they can accept a classical musician."

"Martha's right," Henry said. "People will sense what's in your heart, and if the music speaks to you, you'll be fine. 'Course you've got to be good, but from what I heard at Halligan's that shouldn't be a problem."

"I can't wait to hear you two sing," Martha said. "I've got my ticket."

Jamie handed Henry his change. "Good, I could use some friendly faces in the crowd."

For the next couple of hours, Jamie served up brats, hot dogs and chips while he chatted with people, most of whom said they planned on attending the concert. He wasn't sure he was ready for half the town to be there. He wondered if it was too late to back out. Then he chuckled. As if Emma would let him do that.

Emma. He'd be fine as long as she was there.

After they finished serving lunch, as they were cleaning and packing up, Mick said, "I've been think-ing about the future a lot lately. One day the ranch and the restaurant will be yours."

"Unless there's something you haven't told me, there's no reason to discuss this," Jamie said, trying to keep his voice light despite the tightness in his chest at the thought of losing the grandfather it had taken him so long to find.

"Well, we're gonna talk about it. All I ask is that if you don't want to run the restaurant, you find a reliable manager or sell it to someone who realizes what the place means to this community. Now, the ranch is a different story. If you don't want to live there, at least hang on to it as a place you can come to when you need to get away."

"What about Kimberly?"

"While I love my daughter because she's part of me, we haven't had much of a relationship in quite a few years. I consider myself lucky if she sends me a Christmas card. You're family, Jamie, and to you the ranch and the restaurant won't just be dollar signs. You could have a good life here, you know."

Jamie nodded, not able to trust his voice. He felt a peace here he'd never found anywhere else, and then there was Emma. She'd become so important to him since he'd arrived in Estes Park, but how could he decide about their relationship when he couldn't figure out what to do with his life? Emma deserved better than a guy who was drifting through life without much purpose.

Since he'd arrived in Colorado he'd settled into a routine working at Halligan's and around the ranch. He did his hand exercises. He rehearsed with the band, spent time with Emma and when he wasn't with her, he was thinking about her. The one thing he hadn't done was consider the future.

Just because he was having fun here and enjoyed the challenge of playing country music didn't mean he could have a career. How could he let go of everything he'd worked for? Choosing to leave the Philharmonic would have been one thing, but now he felt if he didn't give it his best shot to get back there, he would be settling.

But hadn't he been telling Emma there was more to life than a career? There was having someone you connected with on that intimate level, and not just physically. There was being part of a community.

As Jamie set out in search of Emma, he was amazed at the size of Pet Walk and the number of booths with vendors hawking everything from pet toys to pet cemetery plots and headstones. Then there were rescue groups, photographers, big-name grocery stores and insurance agents with booths. He'd known dogs and cats were big business, but not like this.

Someone called his name and he turned to see Avery and a tall man walking toward him, a scraggly long-haired dog on a leash beside him.

"So you're the new guy everyone's talking about. I've got to say, I feel your pain," Avery's husband said after he introduced himself. "Until you came along I was the favorite target." Then Reed explained how he'd grown up in Estes Park, but went to school at Stanford and lived in California until not too long ago.

"How long will everyone hold the city stuff over my head?"

"I'll tell you a secret. If people didn't like you, they wouldn't give you a hard time. They'd just smile politely and nod your way," Reed said. "We'll have to get together and commiserate over a few beers sometime."

"We've got to keep you in line, and I'll give you a tip." Avery leaned toward her husband, amusement sparkling in her gaze. "People wouldn't tease you if you quit using words like *commiserate* so often."

Jamie laughed at the pair and the genuine love between them. He was ready for that, for something real and lasting with a woman he could hold on to during life's ups and downs. A picture of him and Emma in his grandfather's living room popped into his head. They'd been so comfortable together, but not in a complacent way. In a way that felt right. A man could get used to having a warm woman to snuggle up with at the end of a long day.

"Thanks again for agreeing to sing at the concert," Avery said. "Emma says you've made a huge difference in the band's sound. I can't wait to hear you two. She's so excited about today and the state fair competition. I hate to lose her at the shelter, but I really hope the band wins. She's worked so hard for so long. No one deserves a recording contract more."

"Speaking of Emma, do you know where she is?"

"Right behind you."

He turned at the sound of her voice, and smiled. Her face held a rosy glow from being outside in the sun all morning. Tendrils of her long dark hair curled around her face. Emma walked over to the dog and scratched him on the head. "I'm glad to see you're behaving yourself this year, Baxter."

"Sounds like there's a story there," Jamie said.

"Another reason for us to get together for beers." Reed smiled.

"I hate to break up the male bonding, but duty calls," Emma said. "Avery, a film student wants to interview you for her project. I told her I'd find you and send you to meet her at the registration tent."

"And I'm off." Avery turned to her husband, a wide grin on her face. "Come on, assistant."

When the other couple left, Emma turned to Jamie.

"Speaking of assistants. If you've got some free time, I could use your help."

"I don't have anything to do until the concert. By the way, judging from what the lunch crowd at the food booth said, half the town's going to be there this afternoon."

"That doesn't surprise me. We've almost doubled our ticket sales from last year."

His stomach rolled over, churning up the brats he'd wolfed down earlier. "Tell me I won't make a fool of myself."

"You act like someone who's never been onstage before, but if you really need reassurance, I'll play along. You'll be fine. I wouldn't let you go onstage if you weren't ready. Now, lucky for you, I've got the perfect cure for a bad case of nerves."

"Oh, really?"

"Yup. Some good hard work."

FOR THE REST of the afternoon Emma put Jamie to work. He tagged along with her, lifting and moving tables. He ran simple errands and kept her company. She'd forgotten what simple companionship felt like. Had she ever really had this with any of the other men she'd dated?

"I could get used to having an assistant," she teased as she and Jamie folded up the tables from the various pet contests.

She could get used to having him around, period. Rehearsals had changed over the past couple of weeks. They still worked hard, but there was a balance in her life, and she realized Avery and Jamie had been right. She'd been shutting herself off from everyone and everything. Now that she'd started opening up, she felt a sense of peace and joy again, and her music was better. More personal. More real. More filled with hope.

"Despite you working me like a pack mule, today's been fun. The best-dressed pet contest was amazing. The work some of the contestants put into the outfits was incredible." He shook his head. "The roaring twenties getup must have taken days to make."

"Avery's going to have to give Mrs. Russell and Chandra a lifetime achievement award or something. It's the fourth year they've won. This year the number of contestants in that contest was way down. I think people are afraid of competing against her."

"That sweet little old lady is scaring off people?"

"I wouldn't compete against her. She's ruthless." Her phone rang. She sighed as she reached into her back pocket. "I wonder what's gone wrong or who can't find what now."

After she glanced at the screen, her gaze sought Jamie's, needing his strength, his reassurance. "It's the doctor's office."

She reached out to clasp his hand. His warmth seeped into her, keeping the cold from consuming her as she answered the call. *Please let me be a match.*

"I am so sorry, Emma. You're not a match," Dr. Sampson said.

Disappointment, fear and blinding pain crashed over her in waves, threatening to level her. She ended the call and with a shaking hand shoved her phone back into her pocket.

"You're not a match." Jamie's voice cut through her haze.

People flowed in and out of her line of vision. The colors of their clothes created a rainbow of colors. An odd buzzing sound rang in her ears. What would happen to Andrew now?

"Come with me, sweetheart." Jamie wrapped his arm around her shoulder, and when he started to lead her away, she followed, too numb to do anything else. Then the next thing she knew they were in a secluded spot behind the large pavilion and she was in his arms crying. Great heaving sobs wrenched from the depths of her.

"I'm so sorry, darling. I know how much you wanted to help Andrew." He kissed the top of her head. "I wish I could make everything right. What about Tucker? Have they heard if he's a match?"

Red-hot rage exploded inside her, obliterating her pain. She stiffened and pulled away from Jamie. "The ass won't get tested."

"You're kidding. How could he refuse to have a simple test to see if he could save his child's life? Did he say why?"

She gazed at the Rocky Mountains behind Jamie. A strong constant presence. So like the man offering his support now. The anger built inside her, threatening to devour her. She started pacing. "All I had was his parents' phone number. When Mark contacted them, they refused to give him Tucker's number. All they'd do was relay the message. The next day they called back to say because of the tour Tucker couldn't deal with getting tested right now."

"Can't or won't?"

She paused. "Exactly. He can't even go in to a doctor's office for a cheek swab? How tough is that?"

The selfish bastard couldn't spare an hour.

"You were there an hour, tops. The selfish bastard won't spare sixty minutes?"

Her heart skipped a beat. There it was again, him almost reading her mind.

"But if he learned he was a match then he'd have to decide about donating bone marrow. I researched it on the internet. He could be in a little pain and stiff for a couple of weeks, but how bad would that be? Is he really that unwilling to reschedule a few concerts?"

"Maybe that's just his excuse. What if he's like Kimberly? What if he's ashamed that he got you pregnant and you two gave the child up for adoption?"

She froze. That thought had never occurred to her. Images were fragile things in the entertainment industry. If the public got ticked off or disillusioned with a performer, it quickly translated to fewer sales and lower ticket revenues. "You may have hit on something. Tucker's worked hard cultivating his image as the honest, hard-working boy next door. If he has to postpone concerts, he'd have to explain why."

"The last thing he'd want to talk about was how he got his high school sweetheart pregnant and dumped her, leaving her to deal with having his baby alone. Not exactly the responsible thing to do. Not that it matters why he won't get tested. The question is what're you going to do about his refusal?"

She knew what she had to do. She had to face Tucker's parents to get his phone number so she could talk to him. He could be the one to save Andrew and someone had to convince him to get tested.

"Let's see his parents say no to me when I'm standing on their doorstep. You can bet I'll get his phone number."

"Atta girl. My money's on you."

She glanced at her watch. "It's already three. Our concert is at four, and I've got to clean up and double-check the stage setup. There isn't enough time for me to talk to his parents now. I'll have to wait until after the concert." She chewed on her lip and peeked up at Jamie. "Will you go with me?"

"If you want me there, that's where I'll be."

Chapter Twelve

Emma hadn't been this nervous for a concert in years, but she wasn't worried about her performance. She glanced at Jamie standing rigid and pale beside her. He'd been doing okay until he'd seen the crowd. She just hoped he didn't pass out.

"Isn't it great? We've never had this many women in our audiences before," Luke said as he joined them backstage.

Yippee. She'd been right. Every man-hungry female within a thirty-mile radius had shown up for their concert. "I'm just warning everybody right now. If women start rushing the stage, you men are on your own. No way am I getting in the middle of a catfight."

Grayson grinned. Luke laughed. Jamie's eyes widened, and though she hadn't thought it possible, he grew whiter. "You really think someone would do that?"

"Breathe or you're going to pass out." She placed her hand on his arm. Muscles flexed under her palm. "It's going to be fine."

"Don't worry, Jamie. I'll throw myself in the path of any women who make it to the stage," Grayson said.

"Thanks for the sacrifice." Emma rolled her eyes. "No one's going to rush the stage. Quit trying to jerk Jamie's chain."

Over the loudspeakers, she heard Avery ask, "How's everyone doing today?"

The crowd cheered and Emma mentally ran through the program one last time. Beside her, Jamie stiffened. She slipped her hand in his and squeezed. "Don't be nervous. You'll be great. Pretend we're back in the garage. Just us. Now put on a big smile. It's showtime."

She walked onto the stage and adrenaline flooded her system. This was where she was meant to be. This was where she belonged. With Jamie. Where she felt comfortable. She greeted the crowd and they cheered back at her. She counted out two measures and the band started playing.

Music flowed out of her guitar, swirling around her, soothing her soul. Jamie's fiddle joined in. The cheers and whistles grew deafening for a few seconds. Out of the corner of her eye she caught sight of him. He appeared more relaxed now, more in his element. She drifted toward him. Her gaze locked with his. The words of the first song she'd written about her son poured out of her, how she may never see him again but she'd always love him, and she felt pulled to the man beside her.

I'm standing at the edge of a cliff about to take the last step, but oh, what a way to go.

As Emma walked off the stage, she realized she'd been smart to wait to talk to Tucker's parents. After a concert she always felt energized, as though she could take on the world. Between that feeling and having Jamie next to her, she could handle facing them. He wouldn't let her fall apart. She almost laughed. That wasn't what she was worried about. Her bigger concern was she'd go postal if they gave her any lip, and then who knows what felony she'd commit. Jamie would help keep her under control. He wouldn't let anything happen to her.

Those thoughts sent a wave of panic through her. When had she started relying on him? Counting on him being there the way he'd been when she'd gotten the phone call about not being a match. She hadn't needed to ask. He'd seen that she needed him and was there for her. Offering his strength, his support.

"That was amazing. Talk about a rush. We've never sounded like that before. Did you hear those women screaming? There was a pretty little blonde in the second row who couldn't keep her eyes off me." Luke hooked his thumbs in his belt loops. "I could get used to this."

"We should go out and celebrate," Grayson said. "I know we agreed not to socialize, but we spend so much time together. Seems silly that we're almost strangers."

Somehow it did.

"I wish I could go out, but there's something I have to do." Emma realized Grayson was right. He and Luke were a huge part of her life and it was time she treated them that way. She explained about Andrew needing a bone marrow transplant, how she wasn't a match and how she hoped to convince Tucker to get tested.

"Give 'em hell, Emma," Luke said.

"They aren't going to know what hit 'em," Grayson added.

Incredibly touched by their support, she thanked them and said she'd see them at rehearsal tomorrow. Once Luke and Grayson left, she turned to Jamie. "You're still willing to go with me to talk to Tucker's family, aren't you?"

He glared at her as if he were insulted by her question. Had she ever had anyone offer her such unconditional support before?

"I'll warn you, this won't be pleasant. I'd put talking to Tucker's parents on my to-do list right behind jumping out of an airplane with a secondhand parachute."

"Walk with me. You need to clear your head before you see them," Jamie said.

She nodded, knowing he was right. Instead of heading toward the parking lot, she turned onto the path to their right. "When I decided to give the baby up for adoption, I needed Tucker to sign the papers. I called his cell but it was disconnected, so I went to his parents to find out how to reach him."

"Talk about history repeating itself."

"Exactly. That's what I'm afraid of. They accused me of trying to trap him. They said if it hadn't been for my 'lack of talent and ambition' he would have landed a recording contract much sooner. They had the nerve to ask me if I was sure the child was his. I told them just because their son was sleeping around didn't mean I was. I came away feeling like I'd been dragged behind a truck for five miles."

"They only have power over you if you give it to them."

"I've never thought of it like that before."

"You are an incredibly talented woman, and you're stronger than anyone I know. You have nothing to be ashamed of."

"You're right, and I'm certainly not the naive girl I was. I refuse to let them intimidate me. I'll do whatever I have to in order to help Andrew."

Grayson was right. They weren't going to know what hit them.

WHEN JAMIE PARKED in the driveway of the large brick house with the immaculately landscaped beds and yard, he shut off the engine and turned to Emma. What a woman. This couldn't be easy for her, not after what she'd told him at the park, and yet here she was. She would go through hell and back for those she loved.

A man couldn't ask for a better woman than that, but what about what she deserved? Forget about that. *Focus on what she needs from you right now.* "Are you sure you want me to come to the door? You're capable of handling this on your own, and my being there could tick them off."

She shook her head before he even finished speaking. "I need you there to keep me from doing anything foolish. I hear stories about people snapping in these kinds of situations all the time. I don't want that to happen to me. I'd look awful in one of those shapeless prison jumpsuits."

Her brittle, nervous laugh rattled through the truck.

"Look at me. You're still the girl that spent hours learning to climb a tree. This may leave you with some scrapes and bruises, but you can do it. You're a survivor. No one can take that away from you. Now screw up your courage and get the job done."

He could have chosen softer words, but that wasn't what she needed. She needed a reminder about her strength and the depths of it to bolster her sagging courage.

She stared at him, her eyes wide with shock. "Geez, warn a girl when you're going to take off the kid gloves."

"I have every faith in you. If you set your mind to something, there's no stopping you."

"Thanks. I needed that."

When her gaze met his, a fire blazed in her eyes. One hot enough to wipe out a national forest in record time.

She threw open the car door, climbed out, slammed

it shut behind her and stalked up the walkway. When they reached the front door, she inhaled deeply, slowly let her breath go and rang the doorbell. A moment later, when a slender blonde woman opened the door, her eyes widened in shock. Then her lips pursed as though she'd taken a big drink of unsweetened lemonade.

She should be afraid. Hurricane Emma was about to make landfall.

"Go away." When the woman tried to shut the door in Emma's face, Jamie shoved his boot in between the door and the jamb.

"You look just like your grandfather, and I see you have his cocky attitude."

He considered defending Mick, but figured why waste his energy? Someone this angry, he sensed this unhappy with life in general, wasn't worth his effort.

The woman turned to Emma. "I'm not surprised you hooked up with another musician. You always were looking to slide by on someone else's coattails because your talent wasn't enough. Now tell him to remove his foot."

He saw the woman's insult hit the mark as pain flashed in Emma's gaze before she could hide it, but she never wavered. "Mary, I want Tucker's phone number."

'Atta girl. Don't give her the satisfaction of seeing she hurt you.

"I can't see as there's any reason for you and my son to talk, but if you tell me what the issue is, I'll relay the information to him."

"That's not good enough. I want to talk to him myself."

"This is about him getting tested to help that boy, isn't it? I told the man who called to get Tucker's number that he couldn't deal with that right now."

Emma stiffened. Her eyes darkened. When she bit her lip, he knew she was trying to hold back her temper, and he wondered if it would be better if she let it loose. At least then she'd get the satisfaction of putting this bitch in her place.

"This isn't just *some boy*." Emma's low, surprisingly calm voice rippled through him, filling him with admiration and respect. "This is your grandson we're talking about."

"No, it's not. He's someone else's grandchild," Mary said. "My son signed away his parental rights. We have no connection with that child. No more than any stranger we see on the street."

This time Jamie was the one who stiffened. The woman's words pierced him, nicking a sensitive spot he hadn't known still existed. This icy detachment, almost to the point of cruelty, had been what he'd run into headfirst when he'd contacted his birth mother.

A realization crashed through him. Some people really did lack the capability for human compassion. He caught sight of Emma out of the corner of his eye. Caring, determination and love for the child she'd never known rolled off her in waves.

"You and your son have a genetic connection with this little boy. Tucker is the most likely person to be a match. Are you saying he won't take a simple test to see if he can help save a child's life?"

"If it were any other time, it would be a possibility, but this tour is important to Tucker's career. Maybe after that's over—"

"Andrew doesn't have time to wait. I want Tucker's number. He owes me for dumping me and moving in with another woman when I was pregnant. Let *him* tell me he's unwilling to help the child we created."

"That may be what you want, but it's not what you're going to get." Mary crossed her arms over her chest and sneered at Emma, as if she was the one who was justified in her indignation.

"You relay *this* message to *your* son. He will get the test done. If he refuses I'll tell whoever will listen, starting with the local media, about his refusal to help *that child,* as you referred to him. Then I'll talk about how the song 'My Heart Is Yours' that he's always been so proud of as the hit that launched his career, was actually something we worked on together and how I've never received a dime for my work. Tell him I'm prepared to sell my soul to the devil to pay for a lawyer to take him to court over that fact."

"You can't do that after all these years."

Emma leaned forward, her posture rigid, her eyes hard and unyielding. "I don't know if I can or not, but let him refuse to have the test, and I'll sure check into it. If nothing else, when I'm done with his reputation, Marilyn Manson will look like a choirboy next to Tucker." Then she turned and stormed off.

Disgust welled up inside him for the woman fuming in front of him. Wanting to drive home Emma's threat, he said, "And if you think you can bully her into keeping quiet if your son still refuses to get tested, let me tell you something. If Emma doesn't tell the media about him, I will, and I won't have to start with the local media. I have contacts in New York. It will be your son's worst public-relations nightmare come to life."

EMMA SAT IN the passenger seat as Jamie drove to her apartment, her arms wrapped around her middle as if she could hold herself together.

"Talk about an unpleasant experience. That rated

right up there with trying on swimsuits." She chuck-led, but instead of a lighthearted sound, it came off al-most fragile.

No. I won't let his mother rattle me. I made it through the battle. That's what counts.

"But you survived," Jamie said, echoing her thoughts. How did he do that? In a few short weeks he knew her better than anyone, except maybe Avery. How had she let that happen?

"You're one helluva woman," Jamie continued. "Tucker Mathis may be a star, but he and his mother can't hold a candle to you. None of his money can buy him what he lacks in character and strength. You've got both by the truckload."

I do, don't I? How had she failed to realize that be-fore? She'd had some tough times in her life, but she'd weathered them. She hadn't given up—on herself or her dreams. That took guts and a whole lot of courage.

"But I didn't get his phone number."

"You accomplished what you needed to, which was making sure Tucker gets tested."

"How can you be so sure?"

"I've seen his family's type before. They're all about image. I guarantee she's on the phone with him right now telling him to get tested. She knew you meant busi-ness about going to the media. There's no way they want the fact that he refused to get tested to save the child he gave up getting out. He'll do whatever's necessary to keep you quiet."

Jamie had pegged the situation after one encounter with Tucker's family. How had she missed seeing what they were like? Basically selfish, image-conscious peo-ple with about as much character as a pet rock.

But Tucker and his family always managed to put

on a good show. His family, prominent and proper, had appeared so perfect from the outside. They were local business people, community leaders who attended church regularly and supported local charities. She'd been young and had only seen what she'd wanted to see. Now she counted herself lucky for having dodged a bullet. If Tucker hadn't walked out on her who knows how many unhappy years she'd have spent with him before things fell apart.

She glanced at the man in the driver's seat beside her. Even years ago, she'd known what a good man Jamie was and he'd only gotten better. Look at how he'd been there for her since he'd come to Colorado. He'd stepped up to help her with the band. He'd been with her through all of this with Andrew.

When he parked in front of her building she knew should thank him, head for her apartment and lock the door behind her. That would be the smart thing to do, but she couldn't bring herself to tell him goodbye. Right now she was so empty and lonely. So didn't want to be alone. No, that wasn't right. She wanted to be *with* Jamie.

"Do you want to come in? I could make dinner or we could order a pizza."

Emma almost cringed. She sounded as nervous as a teenager asking a boy to a Sadie Hawkins dance for the first time.

"You sure?"

The unspoken question hung between them. She didn't care anymore. All she knew was she wanted to be with Jamie, and to hell with common sense.

"Absolutely."

The minute she closed the front door behind her, the shaking started. Something about stepping into her home, her haven, and in that split second she'd let down her guard, the emotions swamped her. Her feelings for Jamie, though Lord only knew exactly what those were, and her fear for the son she loved but had never known. "What if Tucker doesn't get tested? Or what if he does, but he's not a match? Then what will happen?" She dug into her purse for her phone, found the picture Mark had sent her and held it out for Jamie. "This beautiful little boy could die." The boy with her eyes and dark hair.

Tears stung her eyes and strong arms enveloped her, holding her close. She rested her cheek against Jamie's sturdy chest. His strong and steady heartbeat pounded in her ear. She'd shut herself off and quit feeling anything, but now, for good or bad, Jamie had changed that.

She pulled back and gazed into his eyes. His soul lay open, filled with compassion and understanding.

"Hearing what Tucker's mother said had to be hard on you, too. How she referred to Andrew as 'that child.'"

"I got to admit it stung, but only for a second. Some people lack the strength to deal with life. Kimberly's one of those. So is Tucker's mother. For those people there are only two choices—ignore problems or blame someone else. Kimberly ignores. Tucker's mom is a blamer and you're her favorite target." Admiration shone in his gaze. "You're so much better than they are. You meet life head-on. You've been through so much, and yet it hasn't broken your spirit."

"It's come close."

"Close only counts in horseshoes and hand grenades."

She laughed. "I love how you make me laugh."

I love you. The realization rippled through Emma, starting out small but taking root and growing. She waited for the uncertainty, the panic, the fear to come, but instead a calm enveloped her.

Closing herself off from everyone wasn't the way to live. Sure, she'd been protected, but she'd missed out on so much happiness and joy, too. She didn't know where things were going between her and Jamie, but right now she wanted him. She wanted to feel, to grab on to life and hold on for however long she could.

Her hands splayed across his chest, discovering his heart's frantic beating matched her own as she covered his lips with hers. She wanted this man, to have the most intimate connection she could have with another person.

He lifted her into his arms. As he carried her the few feet to the couch, she kissed him with all the passion she'd been holding back. He sank onto the soft cushions, and she moved around to straddle him, the evidence of his desire strong and thick against her pelvis.

Her hands quickly worked the buttons of his shirt and she slid the garment off his shoulders. "My, what broad shoulders and great abs you have," she said, sounding a little too much like Little Red Riding Hood. "Who would've guessed?"

"Must be all that cowboy stock in my genes." He grinned at her. "But I do work out."

With excellent results.

She leaned forward and kissed along his collarbone, but it wasn't enough. Their movements grew frantic as they explored each other. Caressing, teasing, exciting. His hand slipped inside her cotton blouse and under her lacy bra to cup her breast. Her moan echoed in the room.

His lips followed the path his hands traveled, and she couldn't think. The pleasure built inside her, threatening to consume her. Not that she cared. All she wanted right now was Jamie. To be alive and with him.

The sound of her zipper lowering echoed through the room. Then his hand, warm and firm, slid down her abdomen and found her sensitive core. Desire welled up inside her as his fingers stroked her. She closed her eyes and leaned back in his arms. His tongue flicked against her nipple and wave after wave rocked through her, leaving her spent.

WHEN EMMA'S LIPS moved over Jamie's, he knew he should push her away. She was confused. Her emotions had gotten all stirred up. Fear and love for the child she'd never known. Pain over reliving her past with Tucker, and Lord only knew what else. She didn't know what to do about how she felt and she'd turned to him.

Then she kissed him, and he didn't care about anything but her. Giving her what she needed. Pleasing her.

She stiffened in his arms as her body reached fulfillment and he nearly lost control himself.

"While I'm all worn out and satisfied, the same can't be said for you." She cupped him through his jeans, and he groaned. Pleasure, sharp and overwhelming, shot through him. Her palm rubbed against him. He closed his eyes and for a minute he savored the exquisite joy of her touch. The pressure built inside him, threatening to devour him until he knew he'd reached his limit. He clasped her hands in his.

"What's the problem? Is it that you don't have a condom?"

Common sense warred with his raging need. "I'm not going to make love to you."

"Is it me?"

Rejection and embarrassment flashed in her eyes, making him regret the way he was handling this. "No. It's not. You're perfect." His lips covered hers. His need coursed through him as his mouth mated with hers. At some point he'd released her hands and she slid them over his chest. Her fingers teased his nipples, mimicking his early ministrations. Through his haze he heard his zipper lowering. Then a second later her warm hand covered his heated flesh. His moan echoed through the room, bouncing off the walls, threatening to send him over the edge.

His body throbbed and ached in a way he never imagined possible as he pried her hands away from his pulsing flesh. "I want you. There's no hiding that, sweetheart, but a lot's happened within the past couple of days. Your emotions are all churned up, and you don't know what to do about that."

"Oh, yes, I do. I want you. Inside me."

Her words nearly undid him, but somehow he harnessed his self-control. "No birth control's a hundred percent."

Her eyes widened with shock, and he knew she hadn't thought of that. "You're right. I was on the pill when I got pregnant with Andrew." She leaned down and kissed him. Her tongue slipped between his lips and mated with his. When she pulled away, desire flared in her gaze. Her saucy grin taunted him. "That still leaves us a lot of options."

His mind reeled with the possibilities as she pushed him back on the couch. She tugged at his jeans and he lifted his hips for her to free him. Then she straddled him. Proud and passionate, she stared down at him, her dark hair wild and disheveled from his hands. His heart expanded and he swore she could see inside to his soul. He wondered what he'd missed not having her in his life all these years.

Forget about that. She's here now. With you because this is where she wants to be.

She leaned over him, kissing him lightly as her hands skimmed across his chest. Her calluses from years of playing the guitar created an exquisite friction against his heated skin. Then her lips moved lower. He couldn't breathe. When her tongue licked the tip of his sensitive flesh he couldn't hold back his groan, and he forgot about everything but Emma and how she made him feel. Her mouth continued to do amazing things to him until he gave in to the pleasure and the exquisite release.

A few minutes later, once he could think coherently, Jamie wondered what he'd done. Had the most incredible sex of his life with a woman he cared about more than he wanted to admit. That's what he'd done.

He and Emma needed to talk about what had happened between them, about their relationship and the future, but sprawled here with her all warm and softly snuggled against him, he couldn't bring himself to spoil what they'd shared. Especially when he wasn't sure about anything right now. What to do about his career. His life in general. How he felt about the caring, strong woman beside him. She meant more to him than any other woman he'd ever known, but did he love her? How could he say when he'd never felt that emotion for anyone other than his family?

"I don't know what the future holds, none of us do, really, but can we at least say we're dating, and we'll see where this goes?" he said.

"That's fine with me."

Good. They were both clear on where they were and where they were headed.

MONDAY JAMIE WALKED into the restaurant for his shift whistling the tune he and Emma had worked on yester-

day. They'd spent the day together writing music. Then
they'd gone for a mountain hike and talked. About their
childhoods, about college and whatever else came to
mind. They'd followed that with another round of hot
and heavy petting. By far the best weekend he'd had
in a long time.

Jamie headed straight for Mick's office. "I need a
favor."

His grandfather looked up from the stack of invoices
on his desk. "Name it."

"I want to use the restaurant for a couple of hours
on Wednesday before we open to have a bone marrow
donor registration drive. Dr. Sampson's willing to do-
nate his time. He offered his office, but I'm hoping the
turnout will be too big for that space."

"Did Tucker get tested?"

"You're damn right he did." He told Mick how Emma
had stood up to Tucker's mother and threatened to go
to the media if he refused. "She scared him so much
he contacted a local doctor to come to the hotel to take
the sample yesterday. It'll be a few days before we get
the results, but what will happen if he's not a match is
weighing on Emma's mind. I decided to follow her advice of hoping for the best, but preparing for the worst
by organizing the drive."

"That's a great idea. I'll be the first one in line to
get tested."

"I figured we could open up at nine, and be cleared
out in time for lunch."

"Not only can you use the place, I'll give anyone who
agrees to get tested a free lunch."

"That should bring people in. Can I use the restaurant's computer and printer to create flyers to put up
around town?"

"Use whatever you need to. In fact, work on that now. I'll cover your shift around here. Once you've got the flyers printed, put some up in our window, leave a stack on the bar and take some around town. Now get going. You've got important work to do."

AROUND ELEVEN-THIRTY Emma poked her head into Avery's office. "I didn't have anything to bring for lunch today. How about we go out? I was thinking about heading over to Halligan's. I've got a craving for a burger."

Avery laughed. "Sure. A burger. That's why you want to go there. It doesn't have anything to do with wanting to see a certain bartender."

Heat rushed through Emma, leaving her flushed. *Now he's got me blushing. I'm so far gone, but I'm not sure I care anymore.* "I admit that would be an added benefit."

"With as many hours as we've been putting in lately, we deserve a long lunch." Avery grabbed her purse out of her bottom desk drawer. "You and Jamie looked pretty cozy at the Pet Walk."

You have no idea. "We're kind of dating," Emma said as they headed for the shelter parking lot and Avery's car.

"That sounds like you're not sure."

"We're dating. I'm sure of that. What I don't know is where our relationship will go, but for now it's what I need."

She deserved to have some fun and that's what she was doing, but her eyes were wide open. No rose-colored glasses for her. While she loved him, that she couldn't deny any longer, she wasn't expecting a commitment. She was simply enjoying their time together and the fringe benefits of having him in her life for however long it lasted.

"Has Jamie said anything about when he plans on going back to New York? How long is his vacation? Not that he's really had one with all the hours he's put in at Halligan's and with your band." Avery's forehead wrinkled and Emma knew she was thinking about what she'd just said. "Something doesn't add up here. Who goes on vacation and works nearly full-time?"

"You can't tell anyone, not even Reed, what I'm about to tell you."

Avery glanced at Emma and then back at the road. "The look on your face has me worried. What's Jamie done? Is he on the run from the law? What else could be so awful that you have to swear me to silence?"

"Do you agree to keep this to yourself or not?"

"Of course, now spill the story."

Emma explained about Jamie's hand injury and his being let go from the Philharmonic. "He doesn't know how long he'll be here and he wanted to earn his keep. That's his words, not mine. That's why he's working at Halligan's. He's hoping his hand will improve enough that he can return to the Philharmonic or play with another major symphony."

"What about your band?"

"When I asked him to play, we agreed it would be temporary until we found someone permanent, but I kind of forgot to keep looking for someone else. I was having so much fun, and him being in the band felt so right, I guess I didn't want to. Since then we never seemed to get around to talking about the future."

"Don't you think you should?"

"Let me rephrase that. We touched on the subject." She blushed again at the thought of them together in her bed and looked out the window to hide her reaction. "We decided to enjoy each other's company and not worry about the future."

"Promise me you'll be careful."

"I've gone into this relationship with my eyes open, and anyway, I'm not sure I want a serious relationship right now."

That much was true. After the state fair. When she knew whether or not Maroon Peak Pass was good enough to have a real shot in country music, then she could decide about her personal life. Right now she couldn't handle anything else.

A few minutes later they parked in front of Halligan's. When Emma reached the door, she froze. Staring her in the face was a flyer for a bone marrow donor registration event for Andrew. "Avery, look at this. Do you think this was Jamie's idea?"

"It had to be." Avery splayed her hand across her chest, obviously as touched by Jamie's gesture as Emma was.

If she hadn't been in love with Jamie already, this would've sent her falling head over heels.

"He organized this for Andrew."

Avery swatted her on the arm. "He did this for *you* because he cares for you and knows how worried you are that Tucker won't be a match."

Was Avery right? Of course she was. Emma knew Jamie cared about her, but the question was how much. She shoved the thought aside. She'd been raised on a ranch and knew better than to look a gift horse in the mouth for fear of what she'd learn.

"Could we put a flyer in the shelter window, or would we need to get the board's permission first?" Emma asked as she opened the door and stepped inside the restaurant.

"I think in this case asking for forgiveness rather than permission is the wisest course," Avery said. "I'll take some flyers back with us. We can put a stack on the reception desk."

"Good, that'll save me a trip," a familiar voice said from behind them. Emma's heart tripped. She whirled around and hugged Jamie so tightly her arms ached. "This has to be the best thing anyone's ever done for me."

"For a girl, you sure have strong arms." He grunted. "You mind loosening up a little? It's getting tough to breathe."

She let go and stepped back, still stunned over what he'd done. Without her asking. Just to help her. Because he cared.

"I knew you were worried that Tucker might not be a match," he said. "I figured this way we'd have a backup plan."

We.

The simple word worked its way inside her. She and Tucker had been a couple. She'd dated Clint for almost a year, and yet, she'd never had a man think of them as a we before.

Don't go there. Don't start having expectations. Don't count on anything. Hoping for something permanent, wanting more was too dangerous and left her vulnerable.

She knew he hoped to return to the symphony. Mick's words floated through her mind. *He's got a cowboy's heart.* But he'd been raised somewhere else. Why would he want to stay?

Be content with what you have. Enjoy now and say that's enough.

Chapter Thirteen

On the day of the donor drive, when Emma parked in front of Halligan's, she realized she'd been happier the past week than she'd been in years. The state fair competition was this weekend, and Maroon Peak Pass stood a good chance of winning. Her career could really take off, and then there was Jamie. He made life fun again and helped her find the balance she hadn't realized she craved.

If it weren't for Andrew's sickness, life would be perfect. And they were working on that issue. She still had trouble believing Jamie had organized this event. No one ever saw that she needed help and just stepped up to take care of things. Instead, the people in her life expected her to buck up. She was tough. She'd be all right. They didn't need to worry about Emma. She bent, but she never broke.

But having people expect that could be so tiring. Daunting. Like being a superhero without a sidekick to count on.

Until Jamie.

She found him working behind the bar and thought back to when she'd picked him up at the airport. What had the little boy's mother whispered in her ear? *Don't let him get away. There aren't a lot like him left these days*. No, there weren't, but how could she ask him to stay? He had his own dreams, a life in New York. She couldn't ask him to give that up for her. She believed in Maroon Peak Pass, thought they had what it took to make it big, but it wasn't a sure thing. Not like the career Jamie had if he could return to the Philharmonic.

Shoving aside her concerns about their future, she plastered a smile on her face. "What can I do?"

"Nothing. Everything's taken care of."

She strolled around the bar, cupped his face in her hands and kissed him. "You're amazing. Thank you for all you've done."

For Andrew and for me. For shaking up my life.

"We'll find someone who's a match for Andrew today. I know it."

Before she could respond, the front door opened again and Dr. Sampson walked in carrying a large plastic container and wearing a somber look.

Something's wrong.

"What makes you say that?" Jamie asked.

She hadn't known she'd said the words out loud. "Look at his face. That's someone with bad news to deliver. Do you think Andrew's—" She couldn't say the words. Instead she reached out and clasped Jamie's hand, needing his strength and reassurance.

"Can I speak to you alone?" Dr. Sampson said when he reached the bar.

"It's about Andrew, isn't it? He's not d—"

"No, dear. His condition hasn't changed." Dr. Sampson patted her arm. "It's about Tucker."

"He's not a match," she said.

"I'm afraid not. I heard from Andrew's doctor right before I left the office."

Fear washed over her, strong and overwhelming, for

the child who might not grow much older and for the parents who would have to watch him die. She bit her lip to keep it from trembling as she sank into the nearest chair. This wasn't over. She refused to dwell on the negative. Instead she'd remain positive. "Then it's a good thing we're having this drive. I'll pray someone here is a match."

"That's what we're all hoping for," Jamie said. She glanced at the man seated at the table beside her and her heart swelled with love. He'd slipped into her life and filled the void. How would she ever cope with him leaving?

"I can't thank you both for all you've done."

"Now let's get this show on the road," Jamie said.

"You can start with me," Mick said as he settled into the fourth chair at the table. The doctor swiped the swab around Mick's mouth, placed the sample into a tube and handed that to Emma. He nodded toward the marker. "Mark Mick's name on this, and place it in that bin."

Happy to be busy, she saw to the task. "Here's to someone being a match for Andrew."

Please, dear Lord. If I can have nothing else in my life, let me have this one wish.

"I hope we get a good turnout. A lot of people who came into the shelter picked up flyers and talked about coming, but you know how that goes. Everyone says they'll come, but then they forget or something comes up."

Mick patted her hand. "You don't have to worry about that, Emma, girl. We've got a line stretching down the block of folks waiting to get in here."

A line down the block? "I don't know why I'm surprised. This community always has rallied around a cause."

"They're rallying around you. Everywhere I went to put up flyers, people shared stories with me about things you'd done for them over the years. Ways you made them smile or the little things you did for them to help out. They were glad to have a way to repay you."

Beside her Jamie beamed. His hand covered hers and squeezed. "The more people, the better the odds we'll find someone to help Andrew. Now it's my turn."

As the doctor swabbed Jamie, Mick said, "With the line, Doc, I think the smart thing would be for you to take care of any of my staff that wants to get tested before we open the door because I'm gonna need all hands on deck to see to feeding everyone."

Emma smiled at Mick. "Thank you for doing the free lunch deal. I know that has to be costing you a good amount of money."

"It doesn't matter because you're family. You two mean the world to me." He glanced between her and Jamie. Then he cleared his throat and jumped up from the table. "Doc, I'll send the staff out. We don't want to keep anyone waiting too long."

Five minutes later, after Dr. Sampson finished taking samples from the Halligan's crew, Emma opened the front door, Jamie by her side. The first people in line were her father and her brothers.

Since her mother had died, she'd felt a change in her relationship with the men in her family. They didn't know how to deal with her, how to treat her without their mother there. They'd grown distant. Probably because they were guys and it never occurred to them that she might be lonely or need to hear from them. "Thanks for coming."

"We'd have done this sooner if you'd told us about Andrew and that you weren't a match," her father said.

"I shouldn't find out something like that from a flyer in the grocery store window. Someone else might be raising him, but blood's blood."

After she dutifully issued an apology, she introduced her family to Jamie. "Good to see you, son. You, Emma and I need to get together sometime. We could go out to dinner or something."

She couldn't remember the last time her father had asked her to dinner. When they got together it was always because she issued an invitation or came to cook for him. Apparently having a man along made things more comfortable for her father.

Tears pooled in her eyes as she stared at the line of people waiting to get tested. The amount of support and love overwhelmed her as she spotted former teachers and classmates, shelter supporters, nearly everyone she knew in town. As she wiped her tears away, she told herself they would find a match for Andrew somewhere here. The odds had to be in their favor.

AFTER THE MAD lunch rush ended, Emma and Jamie sat at a corner table enjoying their lunch. "I think I need a nap. I'd forgotten how exhausting working in a restaurant could be."

"It's a workout, that's for sure." Jamie's cell phone rang, but he made no move to answer it.

"Aren't you going to at least see who it is?"

"Remember I'm not one of those have-to-be-plugged-in-all-the-time types. I'd rather enjoy our lunch."

A few seconds later his phone pinged indicating he'd received a voice mail. "It was important enough that someone left you a message. Aren't you even curious?"

He chuckled and pulled his cell out of his pocket. "If

I check who called and satisfy *your* curiosity, will you let me eat in peace?"

"I won't dignify that comment with a response."

He glanced at his cell phone, then back at her. "It's the conductor from the Philharmonic. Why would Malcolm be calling me?"

A spark of dread went through her. This couldn't lead anywhere she wanted to go. She forced herself to smile and keep her voice light. "Unless you've developed ESP, there's only one way to find out. Listen to the message."

She stared at the fries on her plate. Apprehension gnawed at her. His conductor could only be calling for one reason, to see if Jamie's hand had improved. And the only reason he'd wonder that was because either the Philharmonic or some other symphony had an opening. Great news for Jamie. Lousy for her.

How could she let him go when she got up every morning and counted the hours until she was with him? When he was such a part of her life? But if she loved him, how could she do anything but let him go?

"He wants to talk to me about an opportunity. Would you mind if I called him back?"

Of course she minded. What she wanted was for him to say he loved playing with her and the band. That he wanted to stay. That he wanted to be with her. For the rest of his life. That he loved *her*. But what about what he needed?

"Call him." She pushed her chair away from the table in the now-deserted restaurant, but his hand covered hers, stopping her.

"Stay."

She didn't think she was strong enough to take seeing his excitement if she'd pegged the situation correctly, but nodded anyway. How could she say no after all the times he'd been there for her?

His face tight with apprehension mixed with curiosity, Jamie returned the call. After exchanging a few pleasantries, he said, "I have, but I don't know if my ability is back to what it was."

He might not realize how much his hand had improved, but she did. If he wasn't back to the level of playing he'd been in the YouTube video she'd watched, he was very close.

"Is he okay?" Jamie paused, and then smiled.

Yup, she'd been right. Someone had an open chair. A numbing cold spread through her body. She'd known this day could come and sworn she'd been prepared for it. Wrong.

"I'm in Colorado. I took a vacation to clear my head. I've been playing with a local country band here. We're performing at the state fair this weekend." Another pause. "I understand. Do what you have to. The earliest I can be there is Monday."

Emma knew what she had to do. She wouldn't let him risk his dream for hers. When he ended his call she said, "Does he have a spot for you or is it another symphony?"

"How did you know?" He shook his head. "Never mind. Sometimes you know me so well it's scary."

Ditto.

"One of the other violinists had a stroke. I thought I had it bad, but this guy's only in his fifties and he's got kids still at home. Talk about rough. Malcolm said he'll survive, but it's going to be a long recovery."

"And he wants you to audition."

Jamie nodded.

"Congratulations. I know this is what you've hoped

for," she said, trying her best to fill her voice with excitement. "The exile has ended. We should celebrate."

He reached across the table, his hand covering hers, and she nearly lost what little control she had left. "That's not how I've seen being here."

Tell me you love me. That somehow we'll figure out a way to make this work for both of us, because I don't think I can bear you walking out of my life.

She thought about what she'd heard from his end of the conversation. "You can't wait until Monday. You need to get to New York as soon as you can."

"I'll take the first flight I can get after the state fair competition."

Today was Wednesday. That meant the earliest he'd leave was late Sunday night. "Malcolm doesn't have a problem with that?"

"He said it's fine."

"I see a *but* in your eyes."

"He's setting up other auditions starting tomorrow."

Time to cowgirl up and do what was right no matter how much it hurt. "You have to get on the first available flight. I know your hand is healed. You can't risk losing this opportunity." She wouldn't let him. When he flashed her his stubborn glare, she changed tactics. "This is what's best for Maroon Peak Pass, too. I've been meaning to talk to you about that. I just hadn't found the right time, and now here it is."

He leaned back in his chair. "This I've got to hear."

"We agreed your playing with us was only temporary. Say we win the contest with you as our fiddle player. Then I have to explain to Phillip Brandise how you aren't a permanent member of the band. That looks unprofessional and could end up damaging our chances with him. If someone pulled that on me, I'd feel deceived and wouldn't trust them. We need to make it or not as we are."

And that doesn't include you.

She bit her lip to hold her emotions in check. She refused to cry. Not now. Not here in front of him. She'd hold it together if it killed her. Then, when she was home, alone she'd fall apart.

She stared at him and hoped he would say that he wanted this dream, that he wanted her, more than anything else.

"Are you sure this is what you want?"

The heart she'd tried so hard to protect shriveled inside her. "It is."

She stood, walked around the table and kissed him. Her lips moved over his, and she tried to file away the memory of his touch. She pulled away and gazed at the man who'd turned her life upside down, who'd taught her to love again. "I wish you nothing but the best." Then she turned and walked out of the bar knowing she loved him more than she'd ever imagined possible, and she had to let him go.

THE NEXT DAY back in New York, back on the Philharmonic stage, Jamie placed his violin in its case. The audition couldn't have gone better. Maybe because he'd temporarily lost his talent, he valued his ability more now that it had returned. The complacency he'd felt when he'd been with the Philharmonic before he'd hurt his hand had disappeared. The joy and sense of purpose he'd felt the first time he played with a major symphony had filled him again. He'd experienced the wonder of classical music, its beauty.

"I'd say if your hand isn't one hundred percent, it's

as close as it can get," Malcolm said. "Welcome back, Jamie."

He waited for the elation to wash over him, but instead he felt torn. How could he enjoy playing both the classics and country music equally? That made no sense. Shouldn't one tug at his soul more? Shouldn't he know what he was meant to do with his life?

But all he knew was nothing made much sense since Emma had walked away from him at Halligan's. He thought they had something together, the kind of connection that didn't come along every day. But she'd walked away as if he'd been nothing more than a quick fling to pass the time.

That hurt, because to him, she'd been so much more.

He was in love with Emma Donovan.

Talk about a complication. The good news was Malcolm thought he'd improved enough to return to the Philharmonic, the bad news was Jamie no longer had any idea if that was what he wanted. "Can I give you my answer tomorrow?"

"I'll give you until noon, but I can't wait any longer than that."

Jamie thanked Malcolm and promised he'd have his answer first thing in the morning. After he left Avery Fisher Hall, the noise and chaos almost assaulted him. People from the nearby subway stop zoomed past him while he stood there trying to figure out where to go. Taxis honked at everyone and everything. The familiar sites of Juilliard, the Met and the other performing arts buildings reminded him of who he used to be.

Who he used to be? He had changed. Things that had once seemed to suit him so well now didn't. Like his apartment. Instead of being a home, the place felt sterile and empty without Emma and Trooper. Right now that was the last place he wanted to be. He thought about his parents. He hadn't seen them in a while. Now their logical approach to sorting out a problem sounded like exactly what he needed.

LATER THAT EVENING, when Jamie walked into the living room with his dad, his mother's gaze scanned him from head to toe from her spot on the couch. "What's wrong?"

"What makes you say that?"

"Are you telling me there isn't something bothering you?" She had that mom look on her face, and he knew there wasn't any point in lying. After he sank into the chair next to her, he explained about Malcolm's call, the audition and his uncertainty. "I have what I wanted. My hand's better, and I can return to the symphony. How come I'm not sure that's what I want?"

"If one of your sisters asked that question, I'd tell her to make a list of the pros and cons of each choice, but you're different," his mother said. "That solution won't work for you."

"Has that been hard on you? Me being so different from Kate and Rachel? From you and Dad?"

His dad's brows knit together in confusion. "What makes you ask a question like that? You weren't any tougher to raise than your sisters. Kids are hard work, no matter who they're like."

"Being different isn't a bad thing, Jamie." His mother reached out to him and placed her hand on his arm. "Now, about not knowing what you want. I suspect that's not true. You're just not sure whether to follow your head or your heart."

"I'm glad one of us is sure. Playing for Malcolm again showed me how much classical music still means to me, but there's something about country music and playing with Emma that calls to me, too." He smiled, thinking of their time together. "She's got so much enthusiasm. It's hard not to get caught up in it. When I'm with her, I don't know. I can't describe how I feel."

"I think you answered your own question," his dad said.

Since he'd left Colorado, he'd felt this hole inside him. As though part of him was gone. Because he wasn't with Emma.

How could he give her up? At the end of his life what would matter more, his career or Emma?

Without a doubt, Emma.

"I love Emma, and I want to be with her, but it's complicated. Her life's in Colorado or Nashville because she wants a career in country music."

"What's this really about?" His mother stared at him with an all-knowing gaze.

What could he say? That he was scared to walk away from everything he'd worked for and basically start over. That he worried they'd resent him for tossing away the education they'd scrimped and saved to pay for. That he feared hurting them by choosing to move to where his birth mother was from?

"Are you afraid we won't approve? That we'll think less of you if you sing in a country band rather than play with a symphony?" his dad asked.

I'm more concerned you'll feel like I'm throwing you aside for Mick, and my link with my birth family. Not able to bring himself to say the words and hurt the parents he loved so much, he said, "You worked so hard to put me through Juilliard, and I'd be giving all that up."

"Nothing's ever wasted, especially education or experience." Compassion and love filled his mother's gaze. "This is your life. We get to live ours. We don't get to live yours, too."

He'd once told Emma he didn't beat around the bush on issues because all it did was cause confusion and hurt feelings, but that was exactly what he was doing now. "I don't want you two feeling like I don't appreciate everything you've done for me. That I'm choosing Mick over you."

"So we've finally gotten to the heart of the problem," his dad said.

"This isn't an either-or situation. Do you remember the song about the penny that Mrs. Hall taught you in elementary school?" his mom asked.

Jamie smiled at the memory. He used to drive his sisters nuts singing that song a hundred times a day when he'd first learned it. "I remember something about love being like a penny, and how if a person held it too tight, he'd lose it, but if he spent it, he ended up having more."

"Just because we love your sisters doesn't mean there's less love for you. We've got room in our hearts for the three of you, whoever you marry and any children you have," she continued. "We know you having a relationship with Mick or living in Colorado doesn't mean you love us any less."

Such a simple concept. Why hadn't he realized that? Now he felt kind of stupid.

"All we want is for you to be happy and find someone who loves you. Sounds like you've found both of those things," his dad said from his seat in his favorite worn recliner.

"If I haven't screwed it up by leaving."

"There's only one way to know."

"She didn't seem too upset when I left." He told his parents about the last time he'd talked to Emma.

"Of course she told you to go," his mother said, a look of confusion on her face as if she couldn't see how he'd failed to realize that. "She did that because she cares about you. Think about it. What would you have done if the situation had been reversed?"

He'd have told Emma to go. In fact, he'd have said whatever he had to in order to make her leave. He'd have wanted her to succeed, to follow her dreams. Is that what Emma had done?

Now he really felt like an idiot. Hopefully it wasn't too late to make things right with her.

AT THE STATE FAIR competition, the longer Emma waited backstage the more her nerves kicked in. At least she'd had good news about Andrew. They'd found out earlier today that her brother Brandon was a match. Now all she had to pray for was that once Andrew had the transplant, his body would accept his uncle's bone marrow.

Today's performance wasn't anything compared to that in terms of life events, but she couldn't help but think how things would be so different if Jamie were here sharing this with her. Without him the band seemed flat. He had a way of bringing out the best in all of them, but especially in her and not just musically. She wanted to share every day with him. Life's blessings and trials.

She had to quit thinking about him.

Like that would happen anytime soon.

"I can't let you backstage without a badge," Emma heard a security guard off to her right say.

"It never fails that someone thinks they can con security into letting him sneak in and grab an autograph," Luke said, pulling her away from her pity party.

"Come on, man. Cut me a break."

Emma froze. She recognized that voice. She heard it every night in her dreams. Only then, when they talked about him leaving, he got down on one knee, told her how much he loved her and said he wanted to spend the rest of his life with her. But Jamie couldn't be here. He was in New York. She'd gone from pity party to completely insane and hearing voices in the blink of an eye. That was the only explanation for what she'd just heard.

"Hot dog. Look what the cat dragged in," Luke said, pointing to his left, his voice full of excitement.

Footsteps sounded around her. Through her haze she noticed Grayson and Luke move past her, but she still couldn't bring herself to look.

"He's with us. You can let him through," Grayson said.

What were the odds that all three of them were having a group hallucination?

If they were, she didn't want to come out of it. *Let me imagine Jamie's here a little longer. At least until he takes me in his arms and kisses me. Then I'll come back to reality.*

But she had to know. She turned and there was Jamie. His cowboy boots clicked on the cement as he strode toward her, dressed in that same brown plaid shirt he'd worn at the fund-raiser concert. The one that brought out the color of his eyes.

Her heart swelled. All she could think of was the line from *How the Grinch Stole Christmas!* about how the Grinch's heart grew three sizes one day.

He stopped in front of her. His index finger flicked the brim of his cowboy hat farther off his forehead. She really should say something, but the words wouldn't form in her head. He'd come back.

"I hear you're looking for a fiddle player."

She reached out and poked him in the chest to make sure he really was here.

"That's an odd response."

"I can't believe you're here."

"In the flesh." Then he grinned in that way that made her heart do backflips.

"Not exactly in the *flesh*."

"We'll see about that later. Now, about that job?"

She leaned back on her heels and eyed him critically. "What experience do you have?"

"Not much with a country band. I was with the Philharmonic, but I quit. I took a long hard look at what I want out of life and that isn't it." Jamie placed his fiddle case on the ground at his feet and clasped her hands in his. "I'm sorry I put you through this. For a while I wondered if I'd latched on to your dream because it was easier than sorting out my own. But I want music in my life, and it doesn't matter what kind because I want you more. I love you, Emma Donovan."

He loved her enough to come back. Tears blurred her vision. "I love you, too. So much. I can't believe you're here."

Jamie thought of when he'd first arrived in Estes Park and how his grandfather had suggested he play country music. The old man had been right after all. Jamie couldn't help but laugh now.

"What's so funny?"

"I was thinking about when I first arrived and how Mick suggested I join a country band."

"That's funny because my grandfather suggested I ask you to play with us before you ever got to town. Do you think they planned all this? That they were playing matchmakers?"

"If they were, we're going to be hearing 'I told you so' forever, but I can live with that." He squeezed her hand. "You still haven't said if I've got the job or not."

She smiled, her heart filled with love and hope for the future. "Cowboy, you can have anything you want."

* * * * *

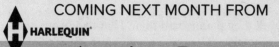

COMING NEXT MONTH FROM

HARLEQUIN®

American Romance®

Available October 7, 2014

#1517 THE COWBOY SEAL
Operation: Family
by Laura Marie Altom

When Navy SEAL Cooper Hansen starts to have feelings for his brother's widow, Millie, he suddenly realizes this might be the most dangerous mission of his military career!

#1518 THE TEXAN'S SURPRISE SON
Texas Rodeo Barons
by Cathy McDavid

Jacob Baron wants to do the right thing for his newly discovered son. But the boy's aunt, Mariana Snow, has her doubts. Can he be the dad his boy needs—and maybe the man Mariana wants?

#1519 HIS FAVORITE COWGIRL
Glades County Cowboys
by Leigh Duncan

Hank Judd can handle his new job as ranch manager and might even survive the arrival of his ten-year-old daughter. Until the woman who broke his heart twelve years ago rides into town....

#1520 A RANCHER'S REDEMPTION
Prosperity, Montana
by Ann Roth

Dani Pettit and rancher Nick Kelly have been friends—*just* friends—for years. But after they share a scorching kiss, Dani can't forget it. Has she ruined their friendship...or discovered she's loved Nick all along?

YOU CAN FIND MORE INFORMATION ON UPCOMING HARLEQUIN® TITLES, FREE EXCERPTS AND MORE AT WWW.HARLEQUIN.COM.

HARCNM0914

REQUEST YOUR FREE BOOKS!
2 FREE NOVELS PLUS 2 FREE GIFTS!

LOVE, HOME & HAPPINESS

Can't get enough of the **TEXAS RODEO BARONS**
miniseries? Read on for an excerpt from

THE TEXAN'S SURPRISE SON
by Cathy McDavid…

"Excuse me, Jacob Baron?"

Jacob turned. The woman looked vaguely familiar, though he couldn't recall where he'd seen her before.

"Yes."

She started toward him, managing to cover the uneven ground gracefully despite her absurdly high heels that had no business being at a rodeo. "May I speak to you a moment?" Her glance darted briefly to his brothers. "Privately."

"We were just heading home," he said.

"This is important."

After a moment's hesitation he said, "Go on, I'll catch up with you."

"No rush, bro," Jet said, a glimmer in his eyes.

"It seems you know my name." He gave her a careful smile once they were alone. "Mind telling me yours?"

"Mariana Snow."

Jacob felt as if he'd taken a blow from behind. "I'm sorry about your sister. I heard what happened."

Leah Snow. That explained why he'd found this woman familiar. Three years ago he'd dated her sister, though describing their one long weekend together as dating was a stretch. He hadn't seen her since.

HAREXP1014

Still, the rodeo world was a small one, and he'd learned of Leah's unexpected passing after a short and intense battle with breast cancer.

"Thank you for your condolences," Mariana said tightly. "It's been a difficult three months."

"I didn't know Leah had a sister. She never mentioned you."

"I'm not surprised." Mariana reached into her purse. "Leah didn't tell you a lot of things." She extracted a snapshot and handed it to Jacob.

He took the photo, his gaze drawn to the laughing face of a young boy. "I don't understand. Who is this?" He started to return the photo.

Mariana held up her hand. "Keep it."

"Why?"

"That's Cody Snow. Your son."

For a moment, Jacob sat immobile, his mind rebelling. He hadn't been careless. He'd asked, and Leah had sworn she was on birth control pills.

"You're mistaken. I don't have a son."

"Yes, you do. And with my sister gone, you're his one remaining parent."

The photo slipped from Jacob's fingers and landed on the table, the boy's laughing face staring up at him.

Look for
THE TEXAN'S SURPRISE SON
by Cathy McDavid,
*part of the **TEXAS RODEO BARONS** miniseries, in*
October 2014 wherever books and ebooks are sold!